W9-BHH-973

THE
MASTER
PUPPETEER

THE MASTER PUPPETEER

KATHERINE PATERSON

Illustrated by Haru Wells

HarperTrophy
A Division of HarperCollinsPublishers

THE MASTER PUPPETEER
Copyright © 1975 by Katherine Paterson
All rights reserved. No part of this book may be
used or reproduced in any manner whatsoever without
written permission except in the case of brief quotations
embodied in critical articles and reviews. For information
address HarperCollins Children's Books, a division of
HarperCollins Publishers, 10 East 53rd Street,
New York, NY 10022.

Library of Congress Cataloging-in-Publication Data
Paterson, Katherine.
  The master puppeteer.

  Summary: A thirteen-year-old boy describes the
poverty and discontent of eighteenth century Osaka
and the world of puppeteers in which he lives.
  [1. Japan—Fiction.   2. Puppets and puppet-plays—
Fiction.]   I. Wells, Haru.   II. Title.
PZ7.P273Mas   [Fic]   75-8614
ISBN 0-690-00913-5

  (A Harper Trophy book)
ISBN 0-06-440281-9 (pbk.)

Published in hardcover by HarperCollins Publishers.
First Harper Trophy edition, 1989.

A Scott Foresman Edition
ISBN 0-673-80146-2

Printed in the U.K.

This book is for my son,
John,
who is part Jiro, part Kinshi,
but mostly his own man.

Acknowledgments

Many people have helped with this book. I cannot name them all, but I would like to say a special thanks to the following:

Mr. Takami Ikoma of the Bunraku Kyokai and Professor Takao Yoshinaga, both of whom were kind enough to read the manuscript, though I am responsible for any inaccuracies that remain. The day with Professor Yoshinaga, among his puppets and precious texts, eating the delicious sukiyaki Mrs. Yoshinaga so graciously prepared, is an experience my daughter Lin and I will always remember.

Mrs. Fusako Fujii and Professor Minoru Fujita for all their help, including the introduction to Mr. Itcho Kiritake, left-hand manipulator of the Asahiza Theatre Bunraku Troupe. And, of course, to Mr. Kiritake for sharing many insights into the life of a modern puppeteer.

Mr. Thaddeus Ohta of the Japan desk in the Library of Congress for tracking down some elusive details of life in Tokugawa times. Here again, any errors remaining are my own.

My husband John, sons John and David, and daughter Mary, who stayed behind while Lin and I spent three autumn weeks in Japan.

Virginia Buckley, who helped us go and who continues to keep me going as a writer.

Elizabeth Branan, who types four-syllable Japanese words without a word of complaint.

The members of the Osaka and Awaji Bunraku troupes who are nourishing the ancient art of puppetry with their lives.

In this book I have not begun to do justice to the complex artistry of the puppet theater. For a good introduction to Japanese puppetry, I recommend *Bunraku: The Art of the Japanese Puppet Theatre* by Donald Keene: Kodansha International, distributed in the United States by Harper and Row and in Canada by Fitzhenry and Whiteside Limited.

CONTENTS

The puppeteers act like the shadow of the doll and become its victim in manipulating it.

—MIYAKE SHUTARO

ONE

Son of Hanji

Jiro shook his hair out of his eyes and bent once more over the worktable. He dipped the brush into the glue and began to apply it to the inside of the puppet head that lay in two halves before him. Jiro licked his lips. He must be careful. The last time he had not put on enough glue, and the head had fallen apart before it could be delivered to Yoshida at the theater. The trick was to put just the right amount, not a stroke too little or too much.

He sighed and dropped the brush back into the glue pot. His big hands—much too big for his skinny thirteen-year-old body—were shaking so that he was afraid a spot of glue would fall on the strings and ruin the works which made the puppet's eyes and eyebrows move. It had taken his father more than two weeks to perfect the mechanism. Jiro grabbed his right hand with his left and commanded it to stop shaking. It was the strong fishy odor of the glue that was upsetting him, he knew. If only he weren't so hungry. What would happen if he ate some of the glue? Would his insides stick together like the two sides of a puppet head?

How stupid he was! If he finished the head properly, his father would paint it, and the puppet would be assembled and sold to Yoshida. By the end of the week they would have some money with which to buy food, and he could stop wondering what glue would do to his belly.

He reached for the glue brush and began, as carefully as his still-shaking hand would allow, to apply glue to the other side of the head.

"You've put too much on it." Jiro jumped at the sound of his father's voice. Hanji, the puppet maker, was kneeling just behind him. The boy reached for a scrap of cloth and was about to wipe off the excess glue when Hanji stopped him. "No, no. Don't use that. Your mother may be able to salvage it for a costume."

"Then what am I to use?" Jiro's voice was shrill, but he hadn't meant to yell. His father hated anyone to lose control of himself.

"Here." Hanji took the brush out of the glue pot and nudged the boy. "Move over. I'll do it." Delicately he flicked the brush across the edge of the pot. "The secret is to get just the right amount of glue on the brush. See? Not too much, not too little."

I know, I know, the miserable boy groaned to himself. *I know all the secrets, all the tricks. I just can't do them with you hanging over my shoulder.*

"Hungry?" his father asked quietly.

"I'm all right."

"It's hard to be hungry at your age. When we sell the puppet, we'll have something better—rice, maybe."

Rice. The thought of rice made Jiro's head feel light. He imagined the smell of it bubbling on the charcoal stove.

"Your mother is back. See if you can help her."

Jiro got to his feet reluctantly. "Can't I help you here?"

"No, not now. I'm finished." Hanji put down the brush and, without touching any of the mechanisms, joined the two halves of the head together, fastening them with a wooden clamp. "Go on. I'll clean up."

Jiro went through the half curtain that separated the shop from the back of the house. The back door was slid open, and he could see Isako on all fours, blowing at the charcoal in the brazier.

"Do you want me to do that, Mother?" He licked his lips, the top lip left to right, and the bottom right to left.

"What? Oh, no. I've almost got it going." She looked up. "Why aren't you helping your father?"

"He sent me to help you."

"What did you mess up this time?"

Jiro blushed a deep red. "Nothing."

"Nothing, huh?" She went back to her blowing.

"Do you want me to get the water?"

"What?" She looked up again, her face pinched with irritation. "You know I can't talk and make a fire at the same time. Yes, yes—get some water. Get anything—just get out from under my eyebrows."

Jiro put the bamboo pole across his shoulders and hung a wooden bucket at each end.

"Don't try to fill them too full."

"No, I won't."

"And don't loiter. It's not safe. And don't keep licking your lips. You look like a stray cat."

It was good to be out of the house. Though it was late afternoon, the sun was still high in the summer sky. There were fewer and fewer people on the streets these days. The poor were too hungry to waste their energy strolling about, and the merchants and those who had a little something feared to go out lest they be robbed by the renegade samurai, the ronin, who had forgotten the code of honor but not how to wield their long curved swords.

His mother would often lament the state of affairs. "Look what we've come to. Where will it all end?" But Jiro could not remember a time when things had been much better.

He was born, as Isako never let him forget, the year of the plagues. Why should he, an unwanted infant, have survived while his older brother and two sisters died? Sometimes he felt that his mother could not forgive him—as though he had sucked their life away in claiming his own.

Now for nearly five years, there had been famine. The Shogun blamed the daimyo, and the daimyo blamed the rice merchants, and the merchants blamed the farm landlords, and the landlords blamed the peasants, who, as they died, blamed the gods.

His family was luckier than most. His father had a skill. Hanji made puppets which the puppeteers could buy because there were still merchants who spent part of their great wealth at the theater. So while with one breath Jiro might curse the merchants who continued to grow fat like vultures on the starving bodies of other men, if it had not been for them, he would have become one more of the starving bodies.

"Please, a little something." An old woman approached him from an alleyway.

"I have nothing, grandmother. I'm sorry."

The old face twisted into a snarl. Jiro broke into a run. No, his mother was right. The streets were not safe. Going down the few stone steps he dipped his buckets quickly into the river and took a roundabout way home.

"It's root tea again," Isako said dully.

"Many medicinal qualities, I understand," Hanji replied. They seemed obliged to carry on this same dialogue whenever they sat down at the table.

"If the two of you would finish that fool puppet, I could get something better."

"Yes, just a few more days. You have the costume all ready?"

"You know I have—since last week."

"The boy and I have trouble keeping up with you, woman. Where do you get all your energy?"

Jiro giggled.

"Will you tell that boy to stop laughing, Hanji? It's not funny. And stop drumming on the table. You'll drive me mad." Jiro began scratching the offending knuckles with the fingers of his left hand. He hadn't even realized that he was beating the table with his knuckles again.

"Don't bother your mother, boy." Hanji downed the last of his tea and turned to Jiro. "I've got just enough coppers for a bath. Want to come?" The boy jumped to his feet.

"Where did you get money?" Isako demanded.

"I had it put aside. It's not enough for food, but a hot bath will take our minds off our bellies for a while. How about you?"

"No, I'll wait until we can afford it." She began to clear the bowls off the low table.

At the public bath Hanji paid the coins to the attendant, who handed them each a basket in which to put their things. Jiro ripped off his clothes and threw them into the basket. His father was taking off his garments slowly and folding them carefully—trousers, tunic, sash, loincloth—and laying them one upon the other. Jiro could hardly contain his impatience.

"It's all right, boy. You can go on in."

Jiro slammed his basket on a shelf and hurried into the steam-filled room, carrying his little wooden bowl with a pumice stone and a towel. He dipped the bowl into the huge tub and drew out some of the hot water, pouring it down over his naked body. How wonderful it felt! He drew more water and began to wash himself with his towel. His father joined him, and they scrubbed each other's backs with the stones, laughing at how dirty they were.

"Shh," said Hanji. "They might try to charge us extra."

Jiro laughed again and poured another bowl of water over his father's back to rinse away the last of the grime. Then they climbed up into the great wooden tub and sat down, the water sloshing around their necks.

"Ahh, hot," Hanji exclaimed contentedly.

"Hanji, is it?" a voice, which they recognized as belonging to a neighbor, spoke out of the steam.

"Yes. Is that you, Sano?"

The two men fell into the kind of gossip one engages in in a public bathhouse—the foibles of friends or neighbors, current events as long as no criticism of the government is implied. There were likely to be more spies in the public bath than rocks in a roadway.

Sano looked carefully around. The room was lit by a few oil lamps, and with the steam it was hard to see farther than a foot away. He sidled over to the puppet maker and his son.

"Have you heard the latest on Saburo?" he whispered.

"No, what?" Jiro thrilled to the sound of the magic name.

"Shhhh," his father warned.

Sano looked about again before continuing. "It seems that early today a funeral procession was going by the door of Furukawa, the rice merchant."

Jiro leaned closer to catch every word.

"Furukawa—that son of a fat blowfish—was standing there on the threshold fanning himself. When suddenly, this lovely little widow faints, right against his bloated body. An old man in the procession begs the merchant to take them into his office until the poor girl can come to her senses. Two hours later one of Furukawa's men hears strange noises and finds him there, gagged with his own sash."

"The funeral procession?" Jiro kept his voice low despite the excitement.

Sano nodded. "They filled the coffin with rice and went on their way, leaving the merchant tied and gagged, spewing poison like a proper blowfish."

"Saburo!"

Sano nodded again. "It must have been. No one else is so clever."

Hanji smiled. "Well, some poor bellies are warm tonight." He stood up.

Jiro got up reluctantly. He wanted to press Sano for more details, or even to hear again some of the earlier exploits of the legendary Saburo, but he bowed his good-bye and followed his father to the dressing room.

Outside, their wooden clogs clop-clopped against the cobblestones.

Jiro felt warm and sleepy from the bath and dreamed, as he walked, about the marvelous brigand. "I wonder what he really looks like?"

"Saburo? Pray you never know. As long as he is only known in a thousand disguises, the authorities will never catch him."

"Is it true that he shares what he steals with the poor?"

"So it is said."

"Then he's not really bad, is he? Even if he is a thief?"

"It is always bad to be a thief, whether your name is Furukawa the rice merchant or Saburo the rogue. But as long as the government does not see fit to punish the one, we must hope that it fails to catch the other."

Jiro twisted around instinctively to make sure there was no one in earshot. Sometimes his father was not as careful as he ought to be.

TWO

The Feast

Hanji laid the completed puppet out in a large wooden box. From the top of its black warrior wig to the legging-bound feet it stretched a full four and a half feet—nearly Jiro's own height. The costume was folded neatly on one side—Yoshida would want to assemble the doll himself. The neck of the puppet rested on the padded wooden shoulder board, and the armature that extended down from the neck had been pulled through the hole in the shoulder board. On the armature were the levers that, when pressed, moved the eyes or raised the hairy eyebrows. The mouth of this warrior was a carved and painted one, though Hanji made puppets with movable mouths from time to time. The arms were attached by string to the end of the shoulder board. The right arm, which would rest on the chief operator's right hand, had the lever on the wrist, but the left arm had a manipulating stick of about a foot long attached to the elbow, and it was here that the lever to move the fingers was placed, for the left-hand operator could not stand as close to the puppet as the chief operator did.

Stiff paper which would serve as the chest and back of the puppet was attached to the shoulder board, and to the lower part of the paper was fastened a bamboo hoop which under the costume would be the hips of the doll. Beside the hoop was a fixed bamboo rod that Yoshida or another chief operator could use to prop the heavy doll when he chose to. The legs hung from the shoulder board. It looked like some kind of strange skeleton lying there, frowning up at Jiro, but it was finished, which meant food for a few weeks, so Jiro smiled back at the scowling face. Gently Hanji covered the box with a large cloth.

"Shall we go?"

"Can I go, too?" His father did not often take him on these trips to the Hanaza. They were for business—not playtime for children.

"Don't let that boy go along. He hasn't swept the kitchen or fetched the water for supper," Isako called from the back room.

"He can do that when we get back. It won't take long."

"He'll forget."

"No, I won't." Jiro followed his father to the front of the house, where they stepped down and slipped into their clogs. "We go only to return," Hanji called out.

"Hurry back," Isako responded crabbedly.

It took them about fifteen minutes to reach Dotombori, the street of entertainers where Yoshida's theater, the Hanaza, was located. It was a street of marvels for the boy. Unlike the other streets of the city it was always full of activity. Gaily dressed ladies, their faces painted, tripped down the street on high clogs, giggling and chattering behind their fans. There were jugglers and magicians offering their tricks to small crowds of onlookers and demanding coins from their audiences but getting few. There were plenty of beggars on Dotombori. Jiro saw one with a baby tied to her back. The tiny head was covered with running sores, and though the baby cried piteously and the old hag grabbed the garments of those who passed nearby, no one paid any heed. There were too

many hungry people to pay attention to any one of them.

"Here we are." Hanji stopped before the Hanaza. The doorway was only a foot and a half high and a couple of feet wide. Yoshida didn't want anyone sneaking in without payment. Hanji called out, "Excuse me! It's Hanji the puppet maker."

A head, which Jiro thought he recognized as that of Mochida, one of the left-hand manipulators, poked out of the narrow opening.

"Hanji. So it is." He drew back in. "Come on in. The master is nearly choked with impatience to get the new doll."

Hanji passed the box through to Mochida, and then he and the boy crawled through the opening. They dropped their clogs on the packed earth of the entrance-way and followed the left-hand manipulator up into the theater. The performance of the day had ended, so it was empty—empty except for the smell of food cooking. Jiro inhaled deeply. *Food.*

"He's growing like a young bamboo, eh, Hanji?" The puppeteer nodded at Jiro.

"So? The woman and I think him small for his age."

"Is that right? Shows I'm no judge of flesh—just the dolls," Mochida replied good-naturedly.

Jiro licked his lips. He wished they wouldn't discuss him. When he realized he was licking his lips again, he ducked his head in embarrassment and followed the men through the empty theater and out a side door near the stage into the west wing that served as dressing rooms and living quarters for the puppeteers.

There they had to make their way through a bustle of men in the narrow hallway, some of whom greeted the puppet maker as they brushed by. Above the busy noise there came a bellow. "You good-for-nothing son of a stinking squid! If you so much as move a muscle, I'll make jelly of your bones."

"Ah," said Mochida. "The master seems to be in the courtyard out back."

Hanji and Jiro slipped on sandals provided at the door and followed Mochida into the courtyard. The two dressing-room wings and the back of the theater surrounded three sides of the cobbled yard, and against the back wall was a kitchen shack, a bathhouse, and a large mud-and-plaster storehouse set sideways into the wall. In the rapidly fading light stood Yoshida, the master puppeteer, a short bamboo rod in his hand. He was facing a boy of nearly his own height, who seemed even taller because of the proud way he held his young shoulders.

"Yoshida," Mochida ventured. "Hanji has come with a puppet for you."

Yoshida seemed to ignore Mochida. Instead he gave a tremendous kick which should have sent the boy before him sprawling to the stones, but the boy, his face set, kept his balance.

"He moved!" the puppeteer bellowed to everyone and no one. "He moved! The doll was to be kept motionless, and this, this assemblage of manure that calls itself a foot operator *moved!*" He gave the boy a swat across the cheek with the bamboo rod. The boy blinked but otherwise did not flinch under the blow. "Get out of my sight! Go sit in a corner and practice keeping still. Do you hear me?" No one could have avoided hearing Yoshida, but he repeated himself. "Do you hear me?"

The boy nodded a sort of a bow and walked, his head erect, past where Jiro was standing into the west wing of dressing rooms. Jiro watched him go until he disappeared through the doorway. What a person he must be! He had not exactly defied the foul-tempered master puppeteer, but then again . . . .

"Now," said the puppeteer in an ordinary tone of voice as he turned his attention to his guests. "What have you brought us, Hanji?"

Hanji lifted the cloth from the box that Mochida was still carrying.

"Humph," said Yoshida, studying the puppet carefully. "Bring it along to my quarters. I want to try it on my hands before I pay you."

The puppet maker bowed and stepped aside. The little procession followed Yoshida into the master puppeteer's dressing room in the west wing. Here the rush matting on the floor was old and stained, and though the cushions that Mochida brought out for them to sit upon had once been elegant, the silk was frayed and even patched with coarse linen. It was the smell of supper that lent the place an air of opulence.

Mochida moved a low table to the middle of the room, and as Yoshida carefully unpacked and assembled the puppet, Mochida began to lay bowls and chopsticks upon the table.

Jiro tried to squash the hope that was rising from his belly. Food. The puppeteers had food. Not only that, but they had enough to share. Impossible. In waiting for the day's performance to be over, Hanji had rudely, if accidentally, arrived just at mealtime. Mochida would surely not serve his master until Jiro and his father left. But—but there were places for three at the table.

The men continued their discussion as Yoshida put his hands inside the puppet and, without really watching, began to try out the mechanisms.

The fierce warrior came to life. His eyebrows rose, his right arm went up in a gesture of defiance. His eyes rolled angrily from side to side. Jiro had the uncomfortable feeling that the bushy-browed samurai doll was seeing straight through his skull and reading his greedy desires.

Then Mochida brought in a pot of steaming rice. He was followed by a boy carrying a covered earthenware cooker from which the smell of fish and vegetables escaped and snaked seductively through the room. Mo-

chida knelt and bowed to indicate that the meal was
ready, and then he and the young apprentice withdrew,
leaving the food, the set table, and a boy quite faint with
anticipation.

Yoshida spread the doll out in a corner of the room
and then motioned his visitors toward the table.

"No, no," Hanji objected politely. "We've just
eaten."

"I know it is trash." The puppeteer used polite
language, but it came out too gruffly to sound polite. "But
if you would do me the honor . . . ."

"No, I'm sure it is a feast"—Hanji's head was
bowed—"but we have just eaten, and rude as it seems, we
must hurry home."

Oh, no! Jiro was dying. This was no time for
etiquette. They were starving—at least he was. And the
puppeteer had not only rice but fish and vegetable
soup—maybe even green tea.

"I insist." Yoshida's voice was deep and commanding.
"I will take it as a personal affront if you refuse to eat my
food."

"Ah," said Hanji. "You must not regard it thus. It is
only that . . . ."

"No, but I will be offended . . . ."

"Then pardon our rudeness." Jiro scrambled over the
cushion at the table and plopped himself down on it. He
bowed his head toward the puppeteer. "We humbly
receive your gracious hospitality." He looked up to meet
his father's eyes, wide with shock.

What had possessed him? He must be crazy from
hunger—that was it—in his right mind he never, never,
would have committed such an unpardonable breach of
manners.

For a horrible moment neither man spoke. Then the
master puppeteer laughed, a little too heartily perhaps. At
any rate, he laughed. "Good, good," he said. "Let's

dispense with the amenities. I'm hungry myself." He turned to Hanji, who sat where he had before still stunned by his son's unbelievable boorishness. "Come on, Hanji. Try to force yourself to eat a little of this poor food."

He should have choked on it, Jiro knew. Of all the stupid things he had ever done, this was the worst by any measure. He had completely humiliated his kind father in front of Yoshida—the man upon whom all their livelihood depended. In the old days men had committed suicide for less. Yes, by all rights, Jiro should have choked or at least the food should have turned to dust in his mouth. Instead, it tasted like a heavenly feast. He ate rapidly with his head bowed over his bowl so as not to meet his father's gaze, and as soon as it was empty, he allowed Yoshida to fill it again and again and again. He might as well be punished for a full stomach as a half-empty one.

No sounds came from his father's side of the table. Jiro dared not look up to see if his father was eating. His own noisy slurping of rice and fish soup was the only sound he could hear. At last, to his regret, the earthenware cooker was empty, and he saw Yoshida putting the heavy wooden lid upon the rice pot which must be empty as well. Yoshida clapped his hands, and Mochida appeared with tea.

"It was a feast," Jiro murmured, still not daring to glance at his father.

"A feast," Hanji echoed.

"It was nothing, mere trash," the puppeteer replied. "Hanji," he added suddenly, "this colt of yours surprises me."

"He has no manners." Hanji spoke so softly that Jiro's flesh crawled.

"Ah—manners—they can be taught, but spirit—that is a gift of the gods."

In the stillness Jiro stole a look at his father. The

puppet maker's head was bowed, but Jiro could see that the forehead was flushed either by anger or shame. He quickly dropped his own head.

The puppeteer continued. "Should the day come that he is not needed in your shop, let me know. All a colt lacks is discipline." He gave a short laugh. "I'm somewhat famous in that area."

"You are too kind."

"Never too kind, Hanji, though I have other faults."

Much to Jiro's distress, neither man carried the conversation further. What would he want them to say? He didn't really know. He didn't want to leave home, not because he was particularly happy, but because it was familiar and his father was usually kind. But he had been so hungry, and here at the theater they had food—delicious, body-warming food. The theater would be an exciting life—performing before the rich merchants of Osaka and having them applaud you and, once you had passed your apprenticeship, pay you. But there was Yoshida with his thin bamboo rod—What happened to clumsy apprentices? Sometimes Jiro's father punished him with words or silence, but he had never beaten him. And yet, perhaps if he came to the theater, he would stop being clumsy. Maybe clumsiness went with being hungry and having made your mother unhappy by being born.

As they left the theater, money in hand, Yoshida said, "If you change your mind about the boy . . . ."

Hanji bowed and mumbled something Jiro could not understand. Jiro bowed, too, a spirited bow, he hoped, though never having thought of himself as "spirited" he wasn't quite sure how to play the role.

They walked home in complete silence. Jiro carried the empty puppet box under his arm with the cloth tucked at his sash. He kept trying to think of words that would convey an apology to his father for his terrible manners, but since Yoshida had called him "spirited," he found that all the apologies he framed in his head lacked sincerity. If this spirit of his was a gift of the gods—something he had been born with—*born* with—*Ara! Don't tell my mother,* he pleaded silently. *Don't, please, don't tell my mother. She already hates me. What will she do if she finds I have humiliated you before Yoshida?* Now his remorse was fully sincere, but there seemed no possible words to express the depth of it. His whole body turned cold as though it had been plunged into a bottomless well.

"Let's stop and buy some rice and vegetables for your mother."

"Yes." Jiro's voice was high and pinched. "Yes, of course. She'll be so glad to have a good supper."

And she was glad. She smacked her lips in a most unladylike fashion over every bite. She didn't seem to notice that her husband and son were eating less than she—her husband remembering perhaps that he had already had a full meal that day and her son out of sheer fright at the thought of the conversation that might follow the meal. Jiro kept peeking at his father to see if there was any clue in the man's face as to what he might say. But the puppet maker's face was a mask of serenity.

"Jiro," his mother said, her mouth still full. "I'd enjoy this more if you'd stop tapping your chopsticks against your bowl."

Jiro looked hastily at his father and put the chopsticks carefully down.

When his mother had chased the last grain of rice from her bowl and propped her chopsticks on the tiny carved stand before it, she gave a sigh of contentment. "Ah, that was good."

Jiro jumped to his feet. "I'll wash up," he said. "Just sit and enjoy your tea. I'll take care of everything."

His mother raised her eyebrows. "A little food works miracles."

"I don't mind. I'm glad to help."

"All right, boy, all right." His father's voice sounded a little too patient.

Don't say anything about today. The boy looked into his father's eyes and pleaded wordlessly. *Don't tell her. She'd never forgive me.*

"All right, boy, go ahead." But Jiro could not tell if his prayer had been heard.

He moved the worktable to one side and laid his quilt out on the workshop floor as always. In the back room his parents were preparing for bed as well. He listened intently. His father had not betrayed him yet. His mother had been to the bathhouse and was relating the gossip, punctuated by an occasional "humph" or laugh from his father. Maybe his father was just waiting for him to go to sleep. He sat up quickly. Perhaps by staying awake, he could keep his father from telling her how he had leaped upon the cushion in Yoshida's dressing room and—had he yelled it?—accepted Yoshida's invitation. He was crazy. He must be. Nobody in his right mind accepted an invitation of that sort. *Nobody except me*, he thought miserably. *I am a slave to my belly. Like a stray dog.*

He thought of the admonition of the samurai code. "When you are hungry, pick your teeth." How brave! If only he could be like one of them, starving on a tiny rice stipend from the government, but too full of pride to complain. While he, Jiro, had for no more reason than that he was hungry brought shame to his father. And he might have waited. He knew that as soon as Yoshida paid them, they would have food. But he couldn't wait. Why couldn't he wait? Why couldn't he have waited just a few hours more? And if he himself couldn't understand it, what would his mother think? Ara! He was like a ronin—no pride, no morals—bullying, stealing, even killing a man for a turnip.

"Something came up at the Hanaza today." His father's voice was somewhat muffled, as though he were already lying down, but Jiro's hearing sharpened by anxiety caught every dreadful word.

"Oh?"

"Yoshida took a fancy to the boy."

"Jiro? Why in the world?"

"I don't know exactly. But he offered to take him into the theater."

"You must have misunderstood."

"Oh, no. Yoshida has no skill for indirection. He put it quite plainly."

"Well, you'd never consider it."

"I suppose not. Still . . . ."

"Yes?"

"They seem to have plenty of food there," Hanji said. "Here the boy is always hungry."

"How do you know they have plenty?"

Jiro braced himself. Now it would all come out.

"They're quite careless about it. The smell of cooking fills the whole place."

"That's stupid."

"Hardly wise in these days. And then," Hanji continued, "Yoshida invited us to stay for a meal."

"Only to be polite."

"Well, of course. But still they eat well."

"That's nonsense. No one eats well in Osaka except the rice brokers," Isako said, "and Saburo."

Hanji laughed. "So they say."

"It doesn't take much cabbage to make a big smell."

"No, I suppose not, but still . . . ."

"You sound almost anxious to be rid of the boy."

"Oh, no. It's just . . . ."

"I suppose if he were any real help to you . . . ."

"Oh, he helps me. He can be quite a help."

"Come now, man, the boy has the touch of a water buffalo."

"He's not so bad—just young."

"Well, I wouldn't wish him on Yoshida—you either for that matter except that he is your son. We can always hope that someday . . . ."

"Then you don't think I should consider Yoshida's offer?"

"No more seriously than it was made."

"All right. Then it's settled."

"Sleep well."

Jiro pulled the quilt over his head and stuffed the rice-hull pillow against his mouth. He couldn't let them hear him crying.

THREE

Yoshida Kinshi

One September evening, soon after dusk, a small group of Komuso monks approached the entrance of the rice brokerage of Yamamoto and begged for alms. They wore the traditional basketlike hats from under which they played their flutes so plaintively that the gatekeeper, an emotional man, it was said later, could hardly keep from weeping. He opened the door for them, though he couldn't explain afterward why he had done such a foolish thing, but they were holy men and hungry. Perhaps anyone would have done the same. At any rate, the monks appeared in a few minutes and made their way out of the city. When the clerks found the gatekeeper the next day trussed up like a chicken on a spit, he told how the basket priests, who had seemed so gentle outside his door, had roughly overpowered him once they were within. Inside the baskets were secret compartments into which they stuffed rice and money, and then they put the baskets back upon their heads, bowed deeply, and left him there. He swore he could still hear their flutes an hour or more after they departed.

"Saburo!" everyone whispered. Once more the people's hero had outwitted the wealthy.

In cooperation with the merchants' guild of Osaka,

the daimyo offered a reward of five hundred ryo for information leading to the bandit's capture.

At the puppet maker's shop the money from the warrior puppet was long since spent, and a new puppet was not yet ready. Yoshida had ordered a beautiful young princess, but when Hanji went to deliver it, Yoshida sent it back. "He said there was something cynical about her expression," Hanji explained.

To Jiro the expression looked the way he felt—hungry. How could Yoshida expect his father to work when they were all doubled over with stomach cramps? It was Jiro's own fault though. He knew it. He ate more than either of his parents, and what was he contributing? Yesterday it was a bottle of spilled paint—today he cut a piece of silk too small, and it was ruined. Perhaps his mother could use it for collars or underlayers, his father had said.

His mother wept openly when she saw what he had done, and they had hardly recovered when a messenger came from Yoshida canceling the new doll altogether. Receipts were down, and they would not try the historical drama after all. Okada, the chief reciter, had started work on a new manuscript, a more modern play, which they felt would draw a larger crowd this fall. As soon as they knew what additional puppets would be needed, they would send the puppet maker a revised order.

Isako ceased crying and started cursing. "That bastard son of a ronin. What does he think we eat meantime— wood chips? May he spend eternity as a foot manipulator for the devil!"

"Hush, woman, hush. Times are hard for everyone. He has to do what he thinks will bring him profits. He has many mouths to feed at the Hanaza. There must be more than thirty there. We have only three. We'll manage."

"You take up for that outcast scum."

"He comes from a once noble house."

"You could say the same for certain rats."

Yoshida's message had a different effect on Jiro. It made up his mind. He would take everything into his own hands. He would go to the puppeteer and say that Hanji had sent him. Once he'd entered the theater, his father wouldn't try to get him back for fear of offending Yoshida. And whatever little wages Jiro eventually made, he could give to his parents. His mother might even be proud of that. She might even feel that he had repaid some of his terrible debt from being born and surviving, bleeding their sparse lives like a leech on a starving ox. He would make them happy and proud and ease their old age. He packed his few pieces of clothing and stealthily made his way out the front of the shop.

It was early afternoon, so there was a performance in progress at the Hanaza. Jiro could hear the voice of Okada, the chief chanter, from far down the block. To his delight he even recognized the play. His father used to take him to the theater when he was smaller and in the days before the famine became quite so intense. It was a domestic drama by Chikamatsu Monzaemon called *The Courier of Hell*. Fittingly enough it was a tragedy of a man driven to suicide by his debts. Even seventy years ago when Chikamatsu was alive, the rich merchants must have hounded the poor, goading them to thievery and death.

The doorkeeper was sitting crosslegged on a wooden platform beside the narrow entrance. Jiro recognized him at once. He was the young apprentice Yoshida had been disciplining that summer evening that Jiro had disgraced himself. Now he was eyeing Jiro suspiciously.

"Excuse me." Jiro bowed as politely as he knew how. "I am the son of Hanji the puppet maker. I have business with Yoshida."

"Oh," said the apprentice, "there won't be time to see him today. This performance lasts another four hours, and he will be rehearsing for tomorrow's play when he isn't actually onstage. You picked a bad time."

Jiro's face must have registered his disappointment, because the older boy said kindly, "Is it something urgent?"

Jiro nodded. How could he go home now? And if he wasn't accepted by Yoshida before his father came looking for him, his whole scheme would collapse, to his own disgrace. "I really have to see someone right away."

"By 'someone' you hardly mean me, right?"

Jiro blushed. "Someone who . . . ."

The boy laughed and waved away Jiro's embarrassment. "You can't offend me. I've been a nonperson so long my face is on the verge of dissolving. Go around to the west entrance on the alley and yell. My mother will probably open the door. Ask to see old Okada."

"The reciter?"

"Reciters always like to think they're in charge of everything. He has a rest break coming up, so he can see you right away."

Jiro thanked him. "How is it?" he asked impulsively. "Do you like being in the theater here?"

The older boy shrugged his shoulders. "There are moments when it is not unbearable. I don't mind taking money, for instance."

"But I thought you were already a foot operator."

"Oh, yes. Last summer. After four years of curtain pulling and money taking, Yoshida let me handle feet onstage. But one day it was dusty, and I sneezed. Now I'm back taking money and pulling curtains again. When I die, I will probably be immortalized—Yoshida Kinshi— the world's oldest and most experienced puller of curtains."

"Yoshida?"

"Yes, my father. I wouldn't take his name voluntarily,

believe me." The older boy laughed. "He wouldn't give it voluntarily either—certainly not to me."

Jiro smiled broadly. "I'm very happy to meet you. I'm hoping to enter the theater myself—please be kind to me."

Kinshi grinned. "Good luck. Well, as I said, go see Okada. They say that thirty years ago he was more of a terror than my father, but you'd never guess it now. Maybe blindness makes a man go soft and sentimental. At any rate, you're just his type. He'll have you hired before my father gets through the third act." He paused. "You really want to enter the Hanaza? You're sure?"

"I'm sure."

Jiro ran around the front of the theater down the alley to the dressing-room door. It was locked, but he called out, and soon it was opened by a fat woman. "Shhh! You fool. There's a performance going on."

"I'm sorry," Jiro said contritely, "but I have urgent business with Okada the chanter. I was told I could see him at his next rest period."

The fat woman looked at him closely. "If you're trying to sneak in without paying . . . ."

"Oh, no. I'm the son of Hanji the puppet maker. You can ask Mochida or Yoshida . . . ."

"They're on stage."

"Or Yoshida Kinshi . . . ."

The woman's expression softened, and she stepped aside to let the boy walk in.

"Okada is still reciting," she said. "Want to watch from backstage?"

She led him back through the hallway off the dressing rooms to the side of the stage. From where she motioned Jiro to stand, he could see both the stage and the platform to the right where Okada sat with the samisen player, who accompanied his recital of the story. The script rested on a low lacquered stand, and Okada would reach over from time to time and turn the pages—a gesture all the more poignant when one looked at his obviously sightless eyes. He knew every word of every play by heart, and yet at just the proper moment he would reach over and turn the page.

He had a marvelous old face, Jiro thought, wrinkled and pinkish brown, not unlike a pickled plum. Okada twisted his mouth sideways and with pursed lips imitated the voice of the unlucky hero's old mother, ordering her son to pay the creditor. Beside him the samisen player strummed the ominous chords that hinted to the audience the doom toward which the hero was inexorably moving. But the musician's face remained as impassive as a still pond—his emotions were all drawn from the three strings of the instrument by the large plectrum that he held in his right hand.

Onstage all the operators were in black with black gauzy hoods pulled over frames to hide their faces from view. Which one was Yoshida? There were three puppets onstage—the unfortunate Chubei, his elderly mother, and Hachiemon, the creditor. Each puppet had, of course, three operators. The chief operator was on high wooden clogs making him stand about a half foot taller than his assistants. To one side the left-hand operator worked, coordinating the left hand of the puppet with the head and right hand. And crouching in between was the foot manipulator. But Jiro soon forgot the presence of the men. They became far less real than the dolls, whose tragedy was being played out as Okada's magic voice spun a web of dread about his audience.

The act was over too quickly. The audience was applauding boisterously. Okada raised the script and bowed in a gesture of reverence. Then he and the musician left the reciter's platform. Jiro pressed back against the wall so that the noisy procession of puppeteers could get past. Three boys about his own age moved in quickly to change the scenery for the next act.

The woman was at his elbow. "Okada is in his dressing room now."

Jiro followed her backstage and then out into the courtyard. They crossed it and reentered the sprawling building on the east side of the stage. Here were the dressing rooms of the reciters and musicians. Hanji had once explained to him that they preferred to remain a bit aloof from the puppeteers—a noisy and emotional bunch of workmen, as these artists were said to regard them.

Okada turned at the sound of their entrance. Jiro knelt and bowed his head to the mat. He had some instinctive feeling that the blind man would know, even if he could not see, when any small courtesy was neglected.

"Come in." It was the voice of a tired old man. The magic had evaporated.

"You must forgive me, sir. I'm interrupting you at a very busy time."

"You are young, but not one of us."

"No, sir, I am Jiro, the son of Hanji the puppet maker. Please forgive my rudeness if I speak directly on the business that has brought me here."

"I am not offended by directness, son."

"Will you do me the honor of allowing me to enter the Hanaza as an apprentice?"

"Do you wish to become a reciter or a musician?"

"I lack the talent to do either, sir."

Okada turned his blind eyes directly at the boy. "Is that truth or humility speaking?"

"Truth, sir. I lack humility as well as talent."

Okada began to laugh, a sputtering sound which shook his frail body. "Very well. We'll send you over to Yoshida. He's always looking for spirits to tame. Tell Mrs. Yoshida that I said to feed you, but it might be better to wait until morning to present yourself to Yoshida. He's not always in the best of moods right after a performance." The old man shook his head, smiling. "Now hand me that quilt, will you? I have to take a nap before the next act."

That night Kinshi helped Jiro compose a letter to his parents telling them of his new apprenticeship, and then Kinshi, who had influence over the rest of the boys if not over his own father, sent one of the apprentices to the puppet maker's shop to deliver it.

Kinshi persuaded his mother to give Jiro a second helping of bean soup and shared his quilts with him when the married members of the troupe had gone home and the rest could finally go to bed in their dressing rooms, which also served as living quarters.

Things were going well. Okada had taken him in. Kinshi had befriended him. Of course he still had to meet Yoshida. The terrible thought struck him as he lay there that perhaps his mother had been right. Perhaps his father had misunderstood. Suppose Yoshida did not really want him? How would he react when he learned that old Okada had hired an apprentice behind his back? He shook himself and curled up in a tight ball under the quilt, trying not to think about thin bamboo rods.

Suddenly he sat bolt upright. If he had no talent for reciting or music or puppet making, what would happen when he tried to move in that perfect rhythm of the puppeteer which imbued their dolls with life? He dived back under the covers and soon shut out that evil vision with sleep.

FOUR

The Hanaza

It was Isako and not Hanji who appeared the next day at the Hanaza during the early-morning practice session. Jiro went through the theater to where he had been told she was waiting, and found her standing before the front entrance, small and dried-up looking, his sleeping quilts rolled up and tied to her back.

He had no idea what he should say to her, so he crawled through the narrow entranceway and bowed awkwardly.

Isako began fuming over the sash that bound the quilts to her back. She didn't seem to be paying him much attention. Her hands were shaking so that she had difficulty loosening the large knot over her chest which secured her load. She sniffed through her nose and tore at the knot ineffectually with her thin fingers. Jiro took a step toward her; he wanted to help, though Isako was always a hard person to help.

Isako sensed his movement. "No, no. I'll get it. Don't be so impatient. You've got what you want. You can wait one moment for your poor mother to give you everything she's got. Selfish, selfish child." She shook her head as if to shake away tears, but there were none on her narrow cheeks.

"You don't understand, Mother," the boy pleaded.

"No, I don't understand." She had gotten the knot loose finally and swung the heavy roll of bedding off her back onto the street. "Even while you were still in my womb, I sacrificed for you. From that first wretched year of your life when I lost everything—everything I loved—I devoted my soul to keeping the breath in your bones. Your father and I have always given the best of everything to you."

"I know, that's why—"

"But it means nothing to you. You've never really tried to learn your father's skill. You're not stupid. You could have if you'd tried. It wasn't exciting enough, I suppose, to be a puppet maker. You had to come here to where the applause and the *money* are."

"No, Mother, don't say that. I—"

"It will kill your father. He's not a healthy man—but you wouldn't have noticed. You never knew he was sick, did you?"

Jiro felt ill. "No, I didn't . . . ."

"If I don't curse you, it's because you are your father's only living child, though to you that means nothing, nothing. But"—she folded the sash and jabbed it between the flap of her kimono—"but I curse the day I bore you."

Jiro, quite weak from her attack, watched the small woman go down the street. Her shoulders twitched, and she moved as quickly as her wooden clogs could on the rough street. More than anything he wanted to run after her and throw his arms around her and make her understand, but suppose she shoved him away? He picked up the quilts and crawled back into the theater.

Breakfast soup had already been served in the dressing room for the five boys who lived there when Jiro returned. He put his quilts in the corner of the closet that Kinshi had assigned to him last night and then sat down beside the older boy.

"They want you home?" Kinshi asked, with his chopsticks picking up a square of bean curd out of the soup and plopping it into his mouth.

"No," Jiro murmured. "I don't think so."

"Your mother is upset."

"Yes."

"Mothers make a career of being upset. Anxiety is dearer to them than a full rice bowl." He elbowed Jiro good-naturedly. "Your soup will be cold."

Jiro tried to smile. And, unfeeling wretch that he was, he knew he would be able to get down the whole bowl.

"Before you drown in your soup, my little friend, I want to properly introduce you to the rest of our miserable little group."

Jiro looked up from his bowl. The other four boys were staring at him. "Oh, I'm sorry." He wiped his mouth hastily and put down his bowl.

"The fairly ugly one, there"—Kinshi pointed with his chopsticks—"as you learned last night is called Wada. Next to me, he is the eldest boy. He has a sinister look about him which means you ought to obey him, don't you think? My suggestion is that you do what he says, so long as it doesn't interfere with doing what I say. Right, Wada?"

Wada grunted and went back to drinking his soup.

"Next to the ugly Wada, you will see the fat and handsome peasant face that belongs to Minoru. He is handsome because he was born of a beautiful mother. He is fat because he has committed his life in single-minded devotion to the great and gracious god of the rice bowl. No god has ever been served by a worthier or more loving priest."

Minoru giggled. His smooth face shone with pleasure at Kinshi's teasing.

"And small Teiji"—Kinshi's chopsticks settled on the last boy—"he is skillful of hand, but not of mouth. We are very fond of him, mind you. But in an emergency we don't ask him for explanations, for it takes him from one tide to the next to complete one coherent sentence. Am I unjust, little fellow?"

"N-n-n-no," stuttered the boy, as happy as Minoru to be teased.

"Now, Jiro. We four here are your elders. As elders go, we are not a bad lot, for we have so many elders above us that with the possible exception of Wada we are as squeezed of meanness as a pickled turnip of wine. Nevertheless, it would make us all feel good if you would make a show of obedience, at least for the first week or so. Right, Wada?"

Wada grunted again.

"You mustn't mind Wada. He's practicing to be a Yoshida, but it will take him years to build up enough wickedness in his system. That's why he only grunts—so afraid some of that carefully hoarded meanness will escape his belly before it's fully fermented."

Teiji and Minoru laughed out loud and even the ugly Wada grinned grudgingly. It was easy to see that they all adored Kinshi. And it was not hard to see why. The elder boy had such a way about him. Jiro remembered how Kinshi had stood unflinching under Yoshida's rod.

Jiro smiled happily at his fellow apprentices and then remembered to bow. "Jiro, son of Hanji," he mumbled humbly. "Please be kind to me."

Soon after the boys' breakfast, Yoshida arrived from his house a few blocks away. Jiro had been watching for him, feeling that once this initial encounter was over, he would feel better about what he had done.

"Excuse me, sir." Jiro was standing outside the master puppeteer's dressing-room door and spoke to Yoshida just as he was about to enter it.

"Yes?" In the dim hallway Yoshida did not appear to recognize him.

"Sir, I pray you'll forgive my forwardness . . ."

"What do you want?" Yoshida demanded sharply.

"I—I'm Jiro, the son of Hanji, the puppet maker. Okada has hired me to be an apprentice to you."

"Okada?" Yoshida stamped into his room and sat down on a cushion. "Well, come on in."

Jiro crept across the floor and seated himself facing the puppeteer. "Yes—um—he told me to report to you this morning."

"He did, did he?"

"Yes, sir."

"Oh, yes, now I remember you. You're the one with the appetite."

Jiro bowed his head. He was hot with shame.

"So your father decided to let you enter the theater, eh?"

Jiro nodded dumbly.

"Why didn't he come directly to me? Why Okada?"

Jiro licked his lower lip and then chewed down on it with his teeth. Maybe if he kept quiet . . . .

"Well, never mind. We'll give you a try. You look skinny. The work is heavy here, you know."

Jiro nodded. "I don't mind the work."

"Oh, you will. They all mind working for me," the puppeteer said. "Well—Yoshida Kinshi is the senior among the boys; Kawada Itcho is senior among the eight foot operators; Mochida Enzo is senior among the six left-hand operators; and I am the senior of the five chief operators. There are fifteen chanters and musicians under Okada in the east wing, but they are not your concern. I am your concern. I am the master puppeteer. You must understand that."

"Yes, sir. Yes. I understand."

"You will before we're through. Well, what are you waiting for? The performance starts within the hour."

"Yes. Oh, yes, sir." Jiro backed out of the room as

hastily as he could manage on all fours. At the doorway, he scrambled to his feet, bowed jerkily, and fled.

He found Kinshi onstage with the other boys setting up the scenery for the day's performance. A historical drama was to be presented, but not one of the stuffy ones the merchants found tedious. It was *The Battle of Dannoura.*

"One of Yoshida's favorites," Kinshi informed him. "A great text, and he gets to show off all his best techniques. He loves the 'Torture by Koto' scene."

"Torture by Koto?"

"Don't you know that one? Akoya, who is a courtesan and musician, hides her lover who escaped from the battle, and when the enemy soldiers come looking for him, she says she doesn't know anything about it. One of them wants to torture her and get the information; the other takes pity on her and decides to test her to see if she is telling the truth. He orders her to play the koto, the samisen, and the kokyu. He figures that a sensitive musician is bound to make a mistake if she's anxious and lying. But the girl forces herself to remain completely calm, and she plays the whole concert without an error. So—they think she is innocent and let her go."

"About three years ago my father made a pair of female hands with moving fingers."

"Yes. Those were the hands for the Akoya doll. And you should see Yoshida use them. I'll put you on curtains for that scene. Then you can watch."

"You really admire your father, don't you, Kinshi?"

"I admire Yoshida the puppeteer. It's not the same." An expression Jiro had never seen before came into Kinshi's eyes. "You'd never believe how he doted on me when I was small. He was worse than my mother. And I," Kinshi said softly, "I worshiped him in those days."

At that point Kawada, the chief foot operator, came

in. "I see you boys will be all ready for next week's performance." He smiled, then bellowed, "But what about today's performance?"

The idle chatter stopped at once. Kinshi only spoke to give directions in a curt businesslike tone, which sounded more like that of the elder Yoshida than the boy himself would have liked to realize.

It was time for the performance to begin when Jiro approached Kinshi with a nervous whisper. "How will I know when to pull the curtains?"

"Oh, that's right. You really don't know any of the texts. I tell you what. I'll tell the left-hand operators to give you a nod when they are ready for their entrances. Then you jerk back the curtain, straight—like this." He reached up and pulled back an imaginary curtain. "There's really nothing to it." Jiro's misgivings must have registered on his face because Kinshi gave him a friendly swat. "Don't worry. We all learn here by the honorable path of horrible mistakes."

Jiro winced. That was exactly what worried him most.

He strained his back, trying to appear as tall as possible as he stood just inside the curtain on the left side of the stage. When a puppet with its three hooded attendants waited there for the cue from Okada or from one of the other reciters, Jiro kept his eyes fixed on the hooded figure nearest him, watching for the promised nod. He got the curtain pulled twice without mishap and would have relaxed a bit and watched the play except that the thought struck him that one of the left-hand operators might be capable of forgetting—or worse that he might misinterpret some inadvertent movement of a hooded head.

There was no one waiting in the wings when Akoya began her concert for the inquisitors. Despite his anxiety, Jiro's attention was drawn to the lovely, graceful figure bent over the koto, her fingers apparently plucking the strings. Okada's voice told of her love and of her terror while the samisen player at his side made his instrument sound like a majestic harp. The illusion was complete. Jiro was unaware of the three men in black—he saw only the courageous courtesan intent on saving the life of her lover.

When it was all safely over and Kinshi had congratulated him, the older boy said, "Yoshida was great, wasn't he? Just as I said."

It took Jiro a second or two to recall that it was Yoshida, with Mochida and Kawada, who had brought the doll his father had made to life.

"Yes, magnificent."

At Jiro's request, Kinshi did not again assign him to curtain duty for the time being. He filched from his father's house copies of the texts for the next two plays so that Jiro could memorize them in advance. When Jiro objected to his taking the texts without permission, the older boy laughed.

"You've got a lot to learn, little Jiro. At the Hanaza if you want anything, you must steal it. No one will share any of his knowledge or materials with you. It is not our way. An artist guards his secrets the way a rice broker guards his money. Nothing is ever given away."

"But you," protested Jiro. "What about you? You've helped me from the first night."

"That," said Kinshi, smiling grimly, "merely confirms Yoshida's opinion of me. I shall come to a bad end, fool that I am. Alas!" he said in mock dismay. "The samurai blood that flowed in my ancestors' veins has become more and more diluted the farther we come from the sword bearers. My grandfather, though forced to become a ronin, kept the code and remained a warrior of integrity until his death. My father was not a warrior. Indeed, when he chose to become a puppeteer—in order to eat regularly without actually stealing—he separated himself forever from all that is honorable in our society and made himself an outcaste. But he did it with style. He apprenticed himself to Okada at the Takemoto Theater."

"Okada?"

"Yes, didn't you know? He was a puppeteer before he went blind. A genius according to Mochida. My father became his disciple, determining, I'm sure, from the very first to outdo his master. If Yoshida could not be a samurai, he would at least produce the greatest line of puppeteers Osaka had ever seen. But the blood petered out on him. His only son is a fool, currently masquerading as a puppeteer, to be sure, but how long can the travesty endure? As Mochida with his store of homey proverbs might say: 'The crow who thinks to imitate the cormorant —*drowns.*' " He dragged out the syllables of the word with a melodramatic flourish.

It was Mochida who presided over the boys' early-morning practice sessions. He was unmarried, so he lived in a dressing room at the theater. It was his habit to bustle into the boys' room well before dawn, yank off their quilts, and greet their shivering bodies with a cheerful proverb.

"To the early riser belong the seven advantages!" he sang out one chilly October premorning, throwing open their night shutters.

Kinshi was heard to mutter from under his pillow, "Seven advantages: work, work, work, work, work, work, and work."

Mochida leaned over and gave Jiro a smack on his cold bottom. "You help Wada and Minoru make the fires. Kinshi! Yoshida Kinshi! You and Teiji draw the water and then hang up the legs. We're going to work hard today."

The five boys groped about sleepily for their trousers. They dressed and began to fold up their quilts and put them away into the closets. Kinshi, his eyes still half shut, began mechanically to sweep the mat floor.

"Ara!" exclaimed Mochida. "You are like a bunch of centipedes who have to bind a straw sandal on every foot before you start your journey. Hurry! Yoshida is coming to watch you practice this morning."

The name had the desired effect. Sleepiness vanished. Jiro raced Wada and Minoru to the storage area beside the kitchen where the charcoal braziers were kept. They carried them into the courtyard. Wada, being the eldest of the three, supervised the laying of the charcoal and tinder and nagged as Jiro and Minoru struck the firestones again and again before the first spark ignited. They filled their cheeks and blew and blew until they were dizzy.

At last the stubborn fuel caught fire, and when they had four braziers burning well enough to provide fire for Mrs. Yoshida to start the breakfast and a few live coals for the dressing-room hibachi, the boys ran back to their room, which Kinshi and Teiji had clean and shining. Five pairs of disembodied puppet legs hung in a line from the rafter, and Kinshi and Teiji were already hard at work, making their puppet legs walk or stamp or stand or sit perfectly still, according to Mochida's command.

"No, no, no, Teiji." Mochida gave the boy a light rap with a thin bamboo stick. "The poor fellow looks as bow-legged as you do. He's a warrior, not a comic." Teiji hastened to straighten the legs to a more military stance. "All right, you three, you've lolled about long enough this morning. Quickly now, get in place. The character for today is Watonai in *The Battles of Coxinga*. This is the scene when he is walking on the beach with his wife. Now he's not in military dress, but he's still a soldier and a hero. Don't forget that."

The Battles of Coxinga was not one of the few texts that Jiro had memorized so far. But the story was a familiar one, and by watching the other boys out of the corner of his eye, he managed to keep up while Mochida began chanting the text and beating time with his bamboo rod against the earthenware hibachi next to the cushion upon which he was seated.

From time to time he would jump up and rap a boy on the elbow to indicate an error. Like the other puppeteers he never suggested how an error might be corrected, but he was more gentle than most in pointing out that one had been made.

"This is where he turns. Turn, turn, turn, turn," he began reciting again, and the boys started to execute the turn, their own bodies crouched in the position of the foot operator, stamping their own feet rhythmically to make the sound of the samurai's feet. "All right, all right," Mochida cried. "We'll repeat that part. The turn is what Yoshida will want to see you do."

They must have repeated the turn thirty times. Each time that Jiro sought to make the turn, holding the handles on the back of the legs, he felt the light rap of Mochida's stick. Each time except one. But he had no idea why he hadn't felt it that once, nor why every other time he had earned it. As far as he knew, he was doing it just like the other boys, who were not getting rapped at all. "We all learn here," Kinshi had said, "by the honorable path of horrible mistakes." He didn't mind the raps nearly so much as not knowing what the mistake was. How could he improve if no one told him how to correct what he was doing wrong? Or even told him what was wrong? His father had always told him—or tried to help him understand.

At long last, Mrs. Yoshida stuck her round face through the door, which meant that the boys were needed to help her with breakfast. Jiro could hardly conceal his relief. He rushed out of the room with such eagerness that Wada glared. Who was this new boy trying to impress that he literally ran from practice to kitchen chores?

Breakfast was served for all the unmarried apprentices and operators plus Yoshida, who because he had put his wife in charge of the kitchen, often took his meals in his dressing room rather than at home. Then there was the general cleaning of the rooms, the theater, and the courtyard, which took about an hour. Following this, preparation for the day's performance would begin.

But today there would be no performance. The rice harvests were coming into the city from the outlying districts, and the merchants were so busy outbidding one another for the fruits of yet another slim yield that no one would bother to come to the theater for the next few weeks. In some of the larger theaters, this season became a little spell of leisure, but at the Hanaza it was the signal for Yoshida to work his people harder than ever. He had left the Takemoto Theater ten years before and drawn with him a number of their most talented leads—Okada, in particular. But he had still to establish the Hanaza as a major theater on a par with the Takemoto, which had once had the great playwright Chikamatsu Monzaemon as its writer, or the Toyotake, which had pioneered in the development of dolls that amazed audiences with the variety of mechanical tricks that they could perform. For Yoshida, the mechanical tricks were less important than the purity of the texts, which was one reason—so they said—for his angry departure from the Takemoto when the latter theater felt compelled to try to keep up with the Toyotake in mechanical wizardry. Still, he did not completely despise the so-called tricks, and his interpretation of the "Torture by Koto" was the most highly praised in the city.

"Respect for the Text" might have been the title of the early morning lecture Yoshida gave to the five boys lined up beside the dangling legs of their puppets: "At the Hanaza, we do *everything* better than anyone else, *and* we keep the texts pure. No silly tampering just to get a cheap effect. Is that understood?"

All five heads bobbed in chorus like one of those

cleverly made Chinese-soldier toys run by a waterwheel.

Yoshida seated himself across from Mochida so he could watch the front of the legs, rather than having them somewhat obscured by the rear of the operators.

"Pick up where Watonai sees the bird with his beak caught in the clam shell and execute the turn."

Mochida began the recitation of the text, again beating time with his stick against the hibachi. Yoshida beat time with his stick against the palm of his left hand.

Jiro tried to direct his eyes so that he would not have to look the master puppeteer straight in the face. He imagined that there was a black hood covering his face and that Yoshida could not see him. He easily imagined the feel of that stick upon his arm or back. And he didn't even know what he was doing wrong. He forced himself to concentrate on the sound of Mochida's voice, a poor imitation of Okada's—but none of the puppeteers expected a reciter to waste his time at the rehearsals of the apprentice operators. They were beginning the turn now. *Stamp, stamp, stamp.*

Yoshida leaped to his feet. Jiro cringed despite himself, but Yoshida strode straight past him to the head of the line where Kinshi stood.

"You ant head!" he shrieked. He brought the full force of his rod across Kinshi's left arm. "You've learned nothing! Nothing! Five years in this theater, and you know less than the day you first walked in." He threw the stick at Kinshi and marched out of the room.

Out of the corner of his eye, Jiro saw his friend's face red and set, his hands still on the handles of the puppet legs, his body still crouched in the proper position for a foot operator.

Mochida's chanting continued, and the practice went on as though nothing had happened.

When the practice was over, however, Mochida sent Jiro to the kitchen for a wet towel. He wrapped it around

Kinshi's arm and murmured something to the boy before leaving.

"What did he say?" asked Jiro.

"He said," Kinshi replied in a hard thin voice, "that in this world there are only four things to be feared: earthquake, thunder, fire, and—father."

It was a busy season for the rice merchants and for the tax collectors, who with haste—prompted by the smallness of the harvest, no doubt—arrived from Edo a week before they were expected and demanded the Shogun's portion of each merchant's rice and payment in silver coin for the long trip back to Edo. Imagine the merchants' dismay when another troop of collectors descended the following week and declared the first tax collection to have been a fraud perpetrated by bandits with forged credentials.

"Saburo." The name was on every tongue, and even in the Hanaza, where no one was really hungry, the word was savored and enjoyed. Who was he? Where would he strike next?

The Shogun, unimpressed with the results of the daimyo's offered reward, personally placed a price of one thousand ryo on the head of the bandit known as Saburo. More than two hundred and fifty years earlier, his predecessor, the Shogun Ieyasu, had issued an edict prohibiting the Christian religion. But now, on top of the old notice boards spelling out the penalties for Christianity, reward posters were pasted. At the moment, the bandit Saburo seemed more of a threat to the present order than a stray Christian or two.

FIVE

The Fourth Fearful Thing

November is a dreary time, once the bright skies of autumn have tarnished to gray and the damp cold penetrates the clothes, and the musical cries of the southbound geese are replaced by the honks and coughs of early winter colds. Minoru was always wiping his nose across his face, leaving a perpetual snail trail on his cheeks. Because of his stutter, Teiji seldom spoke to the other boys, and Wada, jealous of Kinshi's obvious preference for Jiro, hardly spoke to Jiro.

So it meant that Jiro was seen to be the special pet of the senior boy, Kinshi, a status that Jiro took no pains to discourage. He was mostly ignored by the other three, except when their work or meals forced them together. Of all the boys, Kinshi was the one for whom he had respect and genuine affection.

Thanks to Kinshi, who regularly "borrowed" the texts for the upcoming performances, Jiro was memorizing the plays as he needed to and no longer had to stand petrified against the backstage wall waiting for a nod from a kindly left-hand operator to indicate at which moment the curtain should be yanked. Someone must have seen his progress, because when the notice was put up for *The Battles of Coxinga*, his name was on it. He was actually to appear on the stage. Well, not appear exactly, as Kinshi explained. He would be hidden by the waist-high apron toward the front of the stage area, but it would be his hand holding the giant cloth clam in which the snipe's beak was caught. Kinshi was to manipulate the snipe. The glee with which the two boys practiced their struggle might have made Wada more jealous than ever, except that his name was also on the notice board. He, in addition to Kinshi, was to manipulate the one-man puppets—the soldiers in the castle scene. It was a complicated play with many entrances and exits, so both Teiji and Minoru were on curtains, and the door was to be handled in shifts by the foot operators when they were not on stage for a particular act.

Jiro was pleased. He could hardly wait for his father to come, delivering new puppets, so that he could share his first triumph as an apprentice. But his father didn't come. All the puppets to be used were already hanging in the dark hallway or were fetched by Yoshida and Mochida from the storehouse at the back of the courtyard and given resewn costumes. There were to be no new puppets for this play. Why couldn't the princess that his father had worked on so hard last summer have been used? What were his parents going to eat this winter?

There was never any free time for the boys at the Hanaza, or Jiro would have tried to see his parents long before. But now his worry lent him the boldness he needed to approach Mochida.

"My father is ill, I think, sir. I've had no recent word, and I'm quite anxious."

"Rich the man who possesses a dutiful son."

Jiro flushed. He was not a dutiful son. But it was just as well that Mochida saw him as such. "If I could go—very early—and get back by the time of the breakfast chores . . . ."

"It means the other boys will have to do your work earlier."

"I'll ask Kinshi. With your permission."

"If Kinshi agrees to cover your responsibility, I won't object."

Kind Mochida. What would they do without the cushion he provided between them and Yoshida?

Jiro hardly slept the following night. He was so afraid he might oversleep and miss his chance to go home. He heard the fire watch going through the streets, knocking his wooden blocks, and calling out the hours. At last it was four, and he crept out so as not to disturb the others. Minoru was lying on his back, one arm flung across his face, snoring like a pig with a stuffed-up snout. What was Yoshida thinking of, hiring a barbarian like that, Jiro wondered, pulling on his trousers. He imagined Minoru as a foot operator wiping his runny nose on the back of a doll's silken garment. Ugh.

He tiptoed toward the door. "Good luck." The whisperer was Kinshi propped up on his elbow.

"Thanks," Jiro whispered back. He added the polite words of one leaving home. "I go only to return."

"Hurry back," Kinshi responded.

By four even in the entertainment district the streets were completely dark except for the pale light of the moon, low in the sky, but Jiro knew the way well. He had come with his father to the Hanaza from time to time through the years and felt no need of a lantern. As he turned off Dotombori, he passed the high wall of the house he now knew to be Yoshida's. Okada's was a few feet farther on, and round about them a number of houses where puppeteers, reciters, and musicians now slept soundly. Even the brothels were shuttered for what was left of the night.

In a strange way he felt that the city belonged to him, for he seemed its only claimant at this hour. Perhaps he should have felt fearful of the ghosts and spirits of the night, which his mother often spoke of, or of the far more real threat of a shadow ready to leap upon him from a dark alleyway to steal his padded cotton vest, even his tunic and trousers. He certainly had nothing else upon him worth stealing. But he was not afraid. Perhaps it was good for him—his new life at the Hanaza. He was outgrowing the fearful stumbling child he had been. Thanks to Kinshi, he was gaining a confidence in himself that he had never had before. Despite his mother's curse, he would become an honor to his father's name. In time his father would be proud of him. In time—he hastened his steps—Was his father really sick? Why hadn't he been to the theater these two months? Surely his anger at the boy had not kept him away. Yoshida was to blame—that must be it. Yoshida was saving money by using only the old puppets. Why should he care if Hanji and Isako starved? His own belly was full. *May he spend eternity as a foot manipulator for the devil.* That had been his mother's curse on Yoshida. Jiro almost smiled. It was really worse than the one she had issued him.

The house was dark and closely shuttered. He went around to the side and vaulted the gate that hung between the side of his house and that of the next-door neighbor. Then he put his head close to the shutters of the back room where his parents would be sleeping.

"Father," he said as loudly as he dared. "Father, it's Jiro." He waited, but no reply came. He rapped on the shutters with his knuckles. "Father, wake up. It's me, Jiro."

There was a sound from inside. "Who?" a male voice, not Father's, asked.

"Jiro, Hanji's son. Who are you?"

As if in reply he heard the steps across the mat floor.

The person had slipped on kitchen clogs. Jiro could hear the scraping across the stones and then the kitchen door shoved aside, and finally there was a crack in the night shutter.

Jiro ran to the opening.

"Jiro? What are you doing here in the middle of the night?" It was Taro, the son of the neighbor, Sano. He pushed the shutter aside and stepped back. "Come in."

"Where are my parents, Taro?"

"They didn't tell you? Your father was sick, and your mother took him to your cousin's farm near Kyoto. I'm just guarding the house while they're gone."

"Is my father very sick, Taro?"

"I don't know. She said it was his lungs and that the country air would be better—more food there, too, maybe. My father had a friend heading down that way with a cart, so your father had a ride most of the way."

"I see."

"He was spitting, he said, a little pink, but not really too bad. A bit of rest and good food and he'd be his old self. That's what he said to my father."

"You mean his lungs were bleeding?"

"Not really that bad—just a little pink when he spit, I think. You know how it is."

Jiro nodded in the darkness. "Well, thanks for your help . . . ."

"That's nothing at all. I'd offer you something to drink, but . . . ."

"No, no. I can't stay. I must be back well before dawn." He started out the door. "If you hear anything from my parents—I'd like to know. I'm at the Hanaza."

"Sure, I know," replied Taro. "Your mother told me. I'll come right up if there's any news. Go in health."

"Yes, thank you. And you."

The darkness no longer seemed friendly. It was cold and damp, and the moon gave less light than it had before. He broke into a run and was back under his quilt at the Hanaza long before Mochida came in to snatch it off.

Although Yoshida regarded himself as a specialist of the female puppet, he occasionally chose to operate the male lead. As Kinshi explained it, in a play like *The Battles of Coxinga*, when Yoshida did the male lead of the warrior, Watonai, he was on the stage almost the whole time. Because of the elaborateness of the sets, Yoshida made the further decision not to alternate this play with a domestic tragedy as he sometimes did, but to offer this single production as long as there was a profit at the box office.

Jiro was glad, for all his excitement, that his initial appearance onstage came early in the play. He crouched behind the wooden apron and held the stick, so that his giant clam rested just at stage level, as Kinshi had carefully coached him to.

Soon Kinshi, his cloth snipe held high above his bent back, came bouncing onstage, the wings of the bird flapping. He circled around a bit, then turned the bird's head downward, as though sighting the giant clam, and swooped greedily down toward its opened shell.

Jiro yanked his string, and *snap*, he had the poor bird's long beak firmly (or so the audience thought) imprisoned. Kinshi flapped his bird's wings and struggled mightily. Okada recited the tale as the warrior Watonai and his wife Komutsu, walking along the beach, happen upon this scene of two creatures determined to devour each other.

Watonai turned—Jiro carefully watched the turn. What was it about the feet that he had not discovered? Ah, that was it, the right foot, the height of the right foot. He had kept it lower, hadn't he? And it moved, like a dance step—the rhythm exactly matching that of the

samisen. Next time, he thought, he would be able to do it to Mochida's satisfaction. Kinshi was right. Whenever one was on the stage, he had to be alert—there were secrets ripe for stealing for any apprentice who kept his senses awake.

After Watonai's long discourse on the parable of the clam and the snipe—like two warring nations destroying each other and laying themselves open to attack from a third powerful force—Komutsu took her long tortoiseshell hairpin and pried open the clam shell, freeing the snipe.

"Toodle-oo," Kinshi whispered as he sailed his flap-winged snipe away. But Jiro never changed his expression. Somewhere Yoshida's piercing black eyes were watching from under his hood.

"You shouldn't fool around onstage, Kinshi. Suppose Yoshida were to hear one of your dreadful toodle-oos. What would he do?"

"Nothing that he hasn't done before, I'm sure."

But it wasn't the snipe's farewell that eventually got Kinshi in trouble. It was a case of stomach grippe that came upon the foot operator Kawada one afternoon durin₁· the middle of the third act. He manfully completed the scene, but it was obvious to everyone that if he should be forced to continue he might bring disaster upon the performance.

"There is no help for it," Yoshida snapped. "Yoshida Kinshi will have to do the feet for the rest of the performance. He's a fool, but he knows the texts and what I expect. None of the other boys has ever worked with me, and the other operators already have their assignments."

"Are you nervous, Kinshi?" Jiro couldn't help but ask.

Kinshi stuck out his bottom lip and shrugged.

"Good luck."

Kinshi gave a half grin and pulled his hood over his head.

Jiro had to take over Kinshi's one-man puppets in the

scenes calling for soldiers, and when he wasn't onstage, he stood beside Teiji at the left-hand curtain. He was ill with anxiety. He elbowed Teiji and whispered, "Kinshi's doing all right, isn't he?"

"As far as I c-c-c-can tell."

That was the problem. How was Yoshida regarding it? The three of them—Yoshida, Mochida, and Kinshi—were to be "breathing as one" at this moment. Was it possible for Kinshi to work so closely with his father? It seemed to be.

"L-l-looks fine," Teiji whispered encouragingly.

Jiro nodded. *Oh, help him, help him*, he prayed to Ebisu or any god who might happen to be listening.

Finally the last battle was fought, and the victorious Watonai stamped from the stage to the cheers and loud cries of approval from the audience. Okada raised the script and bowed for the final time. The performance was over.

Mochida pulled off his hood. As he passed Jiro, he was smiling.

Jiro pounced on Kinshi. "You did it. You did it."

Kinshi smiled. "If only you were my master, what an easy life I'd lead."

It was nearly midnight by the time the boys had cleared up after the evening meal and cleaned the theater for the next day's performance.

"We ought to have something to celebrate," suggested Jiro. "Something to toast Kinshi's triumph today."

"What do you suggest, Mr. Toastmaster?" asked Wada sarcastically. "The charcoal is quite dead. We can't even boil water."

"I know," said Kinshi suddenly, "where I can get some sake." He went to the door and stuck his head into the hallway. "Everyone seems to be asleep," he said in a loud whisper. "I'll be right back." He let himself out.

"Kinshi, *no*," Jiro called, but the senior boy had already gone.

"He's the world's number one fool," Wada shook his head, half in judgment and half in wonderment.

The world's "number one fool" returned shortly with a jug of what all the boys agreed was the empire's number one wine.

Kinshi even persuaded the reluctant Wada to join the lantern-lit revels, and they all laughed as a teacupful of the potent sake raced down Minoru's throat like water into a rain barrel.

"Aah!" The little pig had choked upon it. Watching Minoru's red face, the tears streaming down, Jiro sipped his own cupful very slowly and studied the happy scene. Even shy Teiji was smiling broadly, and as for Kinshi, Jiro had never seen him look so at ease. It was not just the wine—Kinshi had faced a rigorous examination onstage today and he had passed.

"Did Yoshida give you a word of praise tonight?" he asked.

"Yoshida? A bull would sooner give milk."

"B-b-but bulls . . . ." Teiji began.

"I think," said the voice from the doorway, "that is exactly what he means."

They looked up in alarm. "Yoshida," Jiro breathed.

"Somehow the invitation to this party failed to reach me." He leaned over and picked up the nearly empty jug. "To show you that I am not offended, Mr. Kinshi, I invite you to my room at your earliest convenience." He ducked his head in a mock bow. "I am sure the rest of you are tired after your busy day." He picked up the lamp and blew it out. The four of them stayed frozen in position while Kinshi stumbled across their quilts in the darkness. They listened to him walk down the hall until the door of his father's dressing room slid shut behind him.

Jiro lay rigid, straining to hear the sounds from Yoshida's dressing room. The paper door and distance muffled all but a low murmur, and then the talk ceased. It was replaced by a rhythmic *thwack, thwack, thwack, thwack, thwack*. He winced each time. It was his fault for having suggested a toast, but it was Kinshi who was being beaten. It was not fair. Yoshida should have punished them all. He turned over and tried to shut out the sound. *Oh, Kinshi, I'm sorry, I'm sorry.*

At last Kinshi returned and got under his own quilt. He was greeted with absolute silence, which meant that all the boys were lying tensely awake, waiting.

"Kinshi," Jiro whispered at last. "Forgive me."

"It was nothing" came the tight reply.

Jiro could tell by the way Kinshi wore his sash tied loosely the next morning that he was in pain, but Kinshi's eyes said, "Don't talk about it," so he obeyed their silent command.

A white-faced Kawada returned to work, so Kinshi and Jiro were back as snipe and clam. It was as though Kinshi's triumph had never occurred. Except that into the feeling of fear and respect that Jiro had for Yoshida, there appeared a new strain—hatred. It was like a rivulet of hot, molten lava deep within a mountain.

The Battles of Coxinga had a long run. It was about six weeks before the profits began to dwindle and signal Yoshida that it was time to start work on a new production.

Okada, it was said, was hard at work, writing a new play. Rumor had it the hero was a bandit. Jiro doubted that Yoshida would ever endanger his profits by putting on a play that might offend his largely mercantile audience, but to his surprise Kinshi disagreed. "It depends on the text," he said. "If he likes the text, he'll offend the

Shogun himself. Besides, it's set in the sixteenth century. They won't be smart enough to see any contemporary relevance to a two-hundred-year-old story."

It teased Jiro's imagination to picture little wizened Okada dreaming up stories of brave robber barons and dictating them to an apprentice. "Does he just talk the story when he's writing like that?"

"Oh, no," said Kinshi. "I'm told he always sings it. Sometimes whoever's transcribing for him can't understand, but they can't bear to interrupt and ask him to repeat. They've turned over some funny mistakes at times. But Yoshida knows Okada well enough to know the original intent. He can always correct and edit. And of course Okada doesn't need a corrected script for the scenes he recites."

"It's pitiful to be blind."

"Why pitiful? He is a master of reciting and a playwright as well. I think he's a man to be envied. I'd give my eyes for his position—my ears, too, for that matter."

"Don't joke like that."

"I'm not joking."

Okada's play was not yet ready, so Yoshida chose a familiar favorite, *The Love Suicides of Sonezaki*. Jiro was to pull curtains on the right-hand side of the stage, and as before, he was the only member of the company who did not know the text. "Don't worry, I'll get it for you," Kinshi assured him, but Kinshi's last beating still rang in Jiro's ears. Suppose the senior boy were to get caught again.

"No," he said. "This time I'll go."

"You'll do no such thing," Kinshi replied. "If Yoshida were to catch you going through his things, what do you suppose would happen to you?"

"Then I'll work without knowing the text."

"Jiro, you fool. You can't do that. I got the operators

to cover for you in the beginning, but you've been here almost four months now. You're not new anymore."

"I don't understand," Jiro said. "Everybody is new at first. What do people do ordinarily?"

"Well, of course, the men all know the classical texts."

"But the boys, what do the boys do?"

"I don't know." Kinshi blushed. "I've always stolen for ours. Yoshida has kept them stacked by the alcove as long as I can remember. It was easy for me, and it helped the others."

"You yourself told me we were all supposed to learn by the 'path of horrible mistakes.' "

"That's right. But I know how it feels to have Yoshida angry. And I'm as soft as a steamed custard when I see someone suffer. I told you I lack the character for the theater."

During the fourth act of *The Battles of Coxinga*, Jiro, who had no special assignment, usually stood beside Teiji and absorbed all he could from the stage, but that afternoon he murmured something about a stomachache and slipped out of the theater. He could not bolt the alley door behind himself, but he shut it tightly and prayed no one would notice. He walked as casually as he could down Dotombori—someone might take note of him if he ran—and turned into the street that led to Yoshida's house. The gate in the high wall was locked, but taking care that there was no one watching, Jiro climbed it quickly and jumped down into the tiny front garden. The house was latched, but the night shutters, as he had hoped, were open, so the paper doors facing the garden slid aside. He dropped his clogs below and climbed up into the house.

As Kinshi had said, by the alcove with its flower arrangement and hanging scroll, were stack after stack of bound paper texts. Yoshida had already begun sorting out the ones for *The Love Suicides of Sonezaki*. They were right on top. He picked one up, his heart thundering in his chest. Was Kinshi really so nonchalant about stealing his father's property? He wanted to get out in a hurry, but as he turned something about the flower arrangement caught his eye. It was a winter assortment of cattails and dried reeds in a tall, oddly shaped rush basket. The basket was woven, but the pattern on the side was broken, leaving openings at a place on the side, and the bottom was rounded, so that it had been propped against the wall of the alcove to keep from toppling over. It certainly wasn't a proper container. It was more like—yes, that was it—if you turned it upside down, it would be exactly like the basket hat that a Komuso priest wore over his head. Why on earth would Yoshida have one in his house?

SIX

Bad Omens for the New Year

Okada finished the new play just before New Year's. Yoshida provided a copy to each of the five chief operators, himself included, three to Mochida for the six left-hand operators to share, and two to Kawada for the eight foot operators. The boys, as usual, were given nothing, although their names were already on the notice board for curtain pulling and handling the one-man puppets, which Okada had generously sprinkled throughout his play.

Teiji was terrified. "If I m-m-make a mistake, Yoshida'll kill me, and he's got me up for one-man puppets in three d-d-different scenes."

Kinshi slurped in the last of his breakfast soup. "Don't worry, Teiji. I'll get us a text. Haven't I always?" As he said it, he gave Jiro a look that dared him to contradict.

"It's not the same with a new play," Wada argued gloomily. "Yoshida doesn't have texts lying around the house."

Jiro turned to the senior boy. "What did you do the last time Okada wrote a play?"

Kinshi grinned. "I stole Yoshida's personal copy."

59

Minoru slapped his plump thigh. "You're a devil, a real devil. Isn't he a devil?"

"Oh, no," said Kinshi. "Not really. I gave him a chance to memorize it first."

"And he never suspected?" Jiro asked skeptically.

"If he did, he never mentioned it."

"Well, you're not going to try that trick again," Jiro said.

The other boys turned to Jiro, shocked by his assertion, but interested. "Are you challenging the authority of the senior boy?" Wada asked.

Kinshi, too, seemed waiting for an answer. Jiro put down his empty bowl and placed his chopsticks across it. They had no proper chopstick stands at the Hanaza—at least, not for the boys.

"I'm not trying to challenge your authority, Kinshi," he said. "I just think as the newest boy and the one with the least to lose, it would be better for me to take the risk. I mean, Yoshida can hardly demote me now, can he?"

"Suppose he beats you?" asked Minoru.

"Well, I hope I could take it like a man. We've all had a good example of how that should be done." He looked straight at Kinshi, who met his gaze and then looked away.

"Suppose," Kinshi said softly, still looking not at Jiro but toward the sliding doors, "he should turn you out."

Jiro swallowed. "Then I should be out. But I don't think he would. He's more likely to give me a second chance than one of you. All of you have been here more than a year—you should know better. But me—maybe he'll figure that you made me do it . . . ."

"Y-y-you're a brave fellow, Jiro," Teiji said, not without admiration.

"It makes sense," Wada said. Jiro knew Wada would be much happier to see him beaten than Kinshi.

"Minoru?" Jiro asked.

"Sure," said Minoru. "It's your skin. If you're eager to risk it, who are we to say you can't?"

"And Kinshi?" Jiro turned to his friend, whose gaze was now directed toward the floor matting. He was tugging at a bit of loose straw. "Will you give me permission to get the text this time?" Jiro asked him. The senior boy shrugged, a gesture which Jiro read to mean that permission had been granted.

That same day Jiro sought out a slight boy named Tozo, who was an apprentice samisen player and lived on the other side of the theater. Tozo had a lovely, almost feminine face and was said to be one of the most promising of the apprentice musicians. But somehow despite his talent and handsomeness he had so far escaped arrogance, and unlike most of the youths on the east side of the building, was always courteous to the puppet apprentices on the west side.

"I wonder if you could arrange for me to see Okada? He was kind enough to help me enter the theater, and I've never thanked him properly."

"He's been very busy with the new play, lately," Tozo replied. "But I think things are quieter now. At least I can ask for you. Wait here."

In a few minutes Tozo was back with the news that Okada could see him at once. Jiro would have preferred a little more time. He'd hoped to figure out some kind of present to take to the chief reciter, but since fate decreed otherwise, he straightened his shoulders and marched behind his escort.

Okada knelt beside his charcoal hibachi. The night shutters had not been opened, so the room was dark and felt damp.

"Excuse me." Okada turned to face the sound of Tozo's voice. "It is Hanji's son, Jiro."

Jiro knelt and bowed his head to the mat. "I'm afraid I'm interrupting you at a very busy time," he murmured.

"Young Jiro, is it? Come in. Come in." He motioned the boy toward the hibachi. "It's warmer over here."

"Shall I open your shutters?" Tozo asked.

"Oh, the night shutters. Yes, do. It will be gloomy for you sitting here in the dark, won't it, Jiro?"

"No, it doesn't matter."

"You must forgive me. Light and dark are the same to me, you know. Do open them, Tozo. Maybe the light will dry up some of this cursed dampness." He shook his head. "My bones are getting old, you know. They do feel the damp."

Tozo shoved the shutters open, letting in the pale winter sunshine. It was not strong enough to rout much of the damp, but somehow it made Jiro feel better than sitting in the dark. The sightless eyes stared ahead under their drooping lids, but the mouth was smiling and mobile.

"Thank you, Tozo. And do you think you could find us a pot of tea and a bean cake?"

"Please don't bother," Jiro said.

"It's a good excuse. They don't like sending in sweets to an old man like me. I have to think up a lot of excuses." He poked at the charcoal with a pair of metal chopsticks. "Well, how are things going for you over on the west side?"

"Very well, thanks to you, sir. Please forgive me for not coming sooner to thank you formally, but I had hoped my father might be able to send a small gift—"

The old man put up his hand. "What would I do with a gift? It would just burden me on my journey to paradise."

"But I'm sure he wanted to thank you for your kindness to me. Unfortunately . . . ."

"Yes?"

"He's been very ill. Actually he's left Osaka and gone to be with relatives in the country."

"I'm sorry to hear that." Okada stirred the fire and added more charcoal in a neat little mound. "There is too much sickness and suffering these days, isn't there?"

"Yes, sir."

"Just bring it on in, Tozo." Jiro started. He hadn't heard the other boy at the door.

Tozo came in with a tray which he put down on the matting. He took Okada's right hand and placed it gently on the tea pot, then on each of the two cups and then on the tiny plate with three bean cakes on it. He gave Jiro a nod and excused himself.

Okada poured the tea without bending over the pot, his eyes still staring straight ahead. He lifted one of the cups and handed it to Jiro and then pointed at the bean cakes. Jiro was careful to refuse three times, but Okada persisted, so he helped himself.

"Tell me," Okada said, "how is young Kinshi doing these days?"

"Oh, very well, very well." Jiro's mouth was full of bean cake.

"Yoshida is as severe with him as ever, I notice."

"Oh, that."

"I suppose if I had a son, I would do the same. Hard for the boy to understand, though."

"Understand what, sir?"

"See? You don't even understand. How could Kinshi?" He sipped his tea noisily as old men do. "I'm quite fond of that boy."

"Yes, sir. So am I. He's been very kind to me. Although he's the senior boy, he helps all of us."

Okada smiled. "It's hard for someone like you from the outside to understand our way of doing things in the theater, isn't it?"

"Sometimes, sir."

"Who, by the way, is Kinshi stealing the new script from?"

"Sir?"

"You needn't pretend ignorance. He always steals one."

"What—how?"

The reciter lowered his voice to a comic whisper. "I won't tell anyone."

Jiro put down his tea. His hand was shaking so much the tea was swishing madly about the cup. "As a matter of fact, sir, one of the reasons I came today was about the script."

"Oh?"

"I was afraid if Kinshi stole it and got caught . . . . You see lately his father has been quite strict with him. Well, if we got a script right away, we could all do a better job. Kinshi is supposed to handle several of the one-man puppets, and all of us have responsibilities."

"So you just thought you'd come right to me and ask for a text since no one on the other side is going to give you one voluntarily, is that right?"

"Yes, sir, I guess so."

Okada laughed, the wrinkles deepening in his face. Then he leaned forward and whispered as before. "There's an extra one on that stack of things behind you," he said. "But if anyone asks, be sure you say that you stole it. Otherwise you'll get me into trouble with Yoshida. And we can't have that, can we?"

"No, sir. I guess not." Jiro could not tell if the old man was teasing him.

"You guess not, huh?" Okada laughed again. "Well, since you're getting the extra script, I think I'll take the extra bean cake, all right?"

"Oh, oh, yes, sir. Thank you."

Jiro turned to the stack of scripts.

Brush-stroked on the cover page was the title, *The Thief of the Tokaido*. He picked it up. "You are very kind, sir."

"Kind? I didn't know you took it, remember?" He chuckled as though he had made a joke.

"Yes, sir." Jiro rolled up the precious text and stuck it into the flap of his tunic. "Thank you."

"Tell Kinshi to come and see me. He used to run in here often when he was a little boy, but since he's been over on the west side, he never comes."

"I'll tell him."

Jiro bowed his way out of Okada's dressing room and danced down the hall into the courtyard. He had the text. Their troubles were over—at least for now.

The boys were awakened earlier than ever these days, but they were not complaining because the extra hours were being spent getting ready for New Year's. There was a lot of necessary scrubbing and polishing, which the boys did without particular enthusiasm, but in addition there was the food preparation which enabled them to get in a lot of pinching and dipping before Mrs. Yoshida caught on.

"W-w-we're lucky," said Teiji when he and Jiro were working together making rolls of cucumber and vinegared rice in a seaweed wrapping. "There are m-m-many starving in the city this New Year's."

"Why do we always have food?"

"I-I-I said we're lucky."

"But Kinshi says there are bodies in the streets of people who have starved without anyone to bury them." Jiro slashed the knife through the roll and arranged the rice circles in the red lacquered New Year box.

"As long as we have good audiences, w-w-we . . . ."

"I suppose so, still . . . ." Jiro's voice trailed off. Mrs. Yoshida was coming over. She didn't like them to chatter when they were supposed to be working.

"Jiro," she said. "There's someone to see you out front. He says it's about your parents."

Jiro ran across the courtyard and through the theater. Taro had come as he had promised. Jiro's heartbeat quickened, and as he crawled through the entranceway, his body seemed heavy with dread.

"My father?" he asked at once without even a nod of greeting.

Taro bobbed his head. "About the same, it seems. Your mother came back alone."

"Did she ask you to fetch me?"

Taro hung his head. "I told her you wanted to hear, but she said never mind, not to bother you." He looked into Jiro's eyes. "I came anyway. I thought you . . . ."

"Oh, yes. You did right. I asked you to let me know. Well, how is she?"

"Not too good. We're all pretty hungry, you know. I guess it's the same everywhere."

"Yes, I suppose so." Jiro breathed in deeply through his nose. Fortunately, there was no tantalizing smell of cooking escaping from the theater. "Well . . . ," he said. "Thank you for coming."

"Yes." The other boy nodded.

"I'll come to see my mother as soon as I can, but you don't need to say anything to her, all right?"

"All right."

What Jiro wanted to do was to go back to the kitchen and get something for Taro to eat. But he stifled the impulse. If the people on the outside knew there was food in the Hanaza, it might be dangerous.

He nodded, thanked the boy again, and watched him leave. They would have some time off at New Year's. He would go to see his mother then.

The final day of the old year was spent in an orgy of cleaning and preparation. The boys beat the glutinous rice until Mrs. Yoshida pronounced it ready to make into dumplings for the New Year soup and little cakes which could be toasted over the charcoal. They were to have three full days of holiday with lots to eat and no real responsibilities beyond the building of fires and the sweeping out of rooms. "And Yoshida is sick," Kinshi announced with a grin. "He won't be able to join our festivities."

Minoru lay back upon the mat floor. "Then I can eat and drink all I want," he said happily. The thought of a three-day holiday without the eagle eyes and sharp tongue of the master cheered them all, though they left it to the simple Minoru to express their thoughts in words.

For Jiro it meant no troublesome explanations. He knew Mochida would let him leave. He could spend the whole time with his mother—if she would have him.

Mochida gave him permission to go—as soon as he liked the next morning. "But wouldn't you rather wait," he asked, "at least until the first soup of the year is drunk?"

Jiro thanked him for his kindness, but somehow the thought of his mother hungry and alone took away his appetite for the feasting at the Hanaza.

When Mochida came to wake them and send two of the boys out for the New Year's water from the well on the shrine grounds nearby, Jiro was already dressed and folding up his bed quilts. "Teiji! Minoru!" Mochida barked. "A New Year has dawned. Please get the lucky water before it ends." The boys groaned and turned over. Jiro gave them a friendly jab with his toes. "Be kind to me again this year, friends," he said.

"Wait for me at the side door," Kinshi whispered. "I'll let you out and bolt it behind you."

Jiro waited at the door. He blew on his hands and stamped his feet. It was a bitter morning. What was Kinshi up to, to keep him waiting in the cold?

Kinshi appeared from the direction of the kitchen. "Here," he said, "put these under your tunic." He handed Jiro a square kerchief-wrapped bundle and a jug. "It's soup," he said of the jug. "Just heat it up. The rice dumplings are with the other stuff."

"Kinshi, why do you keep on stealing for me?"

"Because"—Kinshi's face wore an air of mock anguish—"instead of brains I was provided with goosefeathers." He patted his head and sighed. "Now," he said, changing his tone, "get going and hurry back. We can't have you missing all the fun." He gave Jiro a slap on the rear.

Kinshi's jug was leaking, and by the time Jiro reached his parents' house, his tunic would be soaked. He felt frozen from the cold. He might have taken the cursed jug out and carried it in his hand except for the people he passed, huddled in the shelter of gateways or in the alleys. It was too dark to see their eyes, but he could feel the stares as he went by. He slowed his walk and tried to act as he thought someone hungry might. It was a long time since he'd been really hungry. He bent over a little and put his hand on his stomach. At least he was still scrawny. He prayed that the smell of the spilled soup would not travel from his body.

The neighborhood was dark and quiet, the house still shuttered. He went over the side gate and to the back.

"Mother!" he called as loudly as he dared. He didn't want to rouse the neighborhood. "Mother!" There was no answer. He tried the back door. It was unlatched, so he pushed it aside and stepped into the kitchen. "Mother?" He slipped off his own sandals and put on the kitchen clogs. There were no quilts down in the adjoining mat room where his parents usually slept. Jiro took the jug and kerchief from his tunic and put them on the kitchen table. He climbed up barefoot from the stone floor to the mat level, poked his head through the half curtain, and peered into the shop. There was no sign of her. Where could she have gone at this time of morning? It wasn't dawn yet and wouldn't be for a couple of hours.

With a mixed feeling of anxiety (could something have happened to her?) and relief (he didn't have to face her quite yet), Jiro lit a lamp and rummaged about in the small bureau until he found an old tunic of his father's. He changed his shirt. There was water in the barrel. Jiro dipped out a little and rinsed the soup from his own shirt. If he put it outside, it would freeze, he decided, so he wrung it out as dry as he could and hung it in the kitchen. Now for charcoal. There was a little. Jiro carried the cooking brazier into the backyard and made a fire, and when the noxious fumes burned off, he carried it back inside and put a kettle of water on.

Then he opened Kinshi's kerchief. Into a wooden box Kinshi had crammed something of all the good things Mrs. Yoshida and the boys had prepared the week before with tea and rice dumplings and some sweets and delicacies he had never seen before. In one corner was a bit of folded cloth. Jiro undid it to find three tiny silver coins. That rascal—that fool—that thief. He would get them both into trouble with this kind of mischief. He'd have to return the money.

"Who are you?"

Jiro turned at the sound of his mother's voice and just in time to dodge a stick of wood that she brought down heavily where his head had just been.

"Mother! It's me!" He hardly recognized her. Her eyes were wild, her hair disheveled, her kimono nearly torn off at the shoulder.

She dropped the wood and stared at him, then swayed, her eyes drooping. Jiro caught her before she hit the stones of the kitchen floor.

He dragged her across the kitchen to the edge of the matting, lay the upper part of her body on the matting and then lifted her legs up. She looked like a paper person, but she was heavy and awkward to handle. He climbed up into the room and got a cushion to put under her head and then a quilt to cover her.

Her eyes began to flutter. She shook her head and shoulders and painfully raised herself on her elbow.

Jiro knelt beside her. "A New Year has dawned. This year, again, I ask for your kindness."

"New Year," she echoed dully and lay back.

Jiro stepped down into the kitchen. The water was ready, so he made a pot of tea and put the soup on to heat. He tried to smile up at Isako as he worked. "I've brought a little feast with me," he said, wanting to sound more cheerful than he felt.

"Food. Where did you get food?"

"Yoshida sent it." He did not specify which Yoshida.

"That outcast bum. He will be lucky to be reincarnated as a cockroach."

"Yes," Jiro agreed happily. His mother was back to her normal self. "But it doesn't hurt the taste of his food," he said.

"I'm going to change my kimono." Jiro nodded and turned his back to give her privacy. "Mine got torn."

"I-I noticed it was a little torn."

"A *little* torn. Those beasts would have torn my arm off."

Jiro stirred the soup. Should he ask her what happened? Would it make her angry if he seemed to pry?

"I see you don't care what happened."

"Yes, I do. I—"

"I was trying"—her voice was tight—"to get a little food."

"Oh," he replied stupidly.

"There was a rumor that food was to be given out at the Ebisu Shrine. Sano told me. The priests were distributing a gift—from Saburo—so they said."

"Saburo?"

"Oh, you know Sano. He always has a tale. There was a big party the night before last for the richest merchants at the house of Kawaguchi. While the city starves, those bloodsuckers gather to dance upon our bones. Well, this time they drank too much—or perhaps, as Sano says, the wine was drugged. At any rate they woke up to find the entertainers all gone—along with the food, their purses, and all of their clothing beyond their loincloths."

"And this was what the priests of Ebisu Shrine were distributing?"

"Who knows? At any rate it was useless—dangerous to go. I received a small packet of food as did Sano and Taro, but as we left the shrine, there was a mob waiting—those who came too late for the distribution."

"Did they attack you?"

"*No, no*. They kissed our sandals and prayed for our continued health in the New Year," she concluded bitterly.

Jiro turned. "I'm sorry they hurt you," he said.

"Sano's son was there to help *him*."

"Yes." Jiro kept his head down as he poured the soup. Without any further words—What could he say that would not bring her anger down upon him?—Jiro climbed up and pulled the low table into the center of the room. He folded up the quilt, and then, putting cushions on either side of the table, served the food.

He could not bear to watch her eat. Isako looked like a mountain monkey on Mount Hiei grabbing at the trash left behind by pilgrims. He bowed his head and drank his own soup very slowly.

"We must not eat it all now," Isako said abruptly. She began in a housewifely fashion to tidy up the box. "What's this?"

Jiro's skin prickled on his scalp. He'd forgotten about the money. "Is there something there?" It was too late to get it back.

"Money," she said. "Where did you get it?"

"I guess Yoshida put it in. Maybe it's a New Year's bonus."

"Humph." She turned the coins over in her palm. Jiro waited for her to say more, but she didn't say anything.

"How is my father?" he asked finally.

"Oh," she said, giving him a bitter look. "How should I know? He needs proper food. There's none to be had, even in the country these days. Except"—she looked at the food box—"except it would seem, in the bosom of the rice merchants and moneylenders of Osaka."

The rest of the day, as he swept the matting and scrubbed the stone floor of the kitchen and courtyard, he made up things to say to her in his head. If, somehow, he could think of the right words, perhaps she would understand why he had gone to the Hanaza and hate him a little less. But the words always shriveled before they could make their way through his dry throat to his lips. He wished that she could know that at the Hanaza he was fairly well thought of—obviously more clever than Minoru and probably the equal of any of the boys, with the exception of Kinshi. And Kinshi—even Wada recognized that Kinshi had made Jiro his special friend. He wanted to tell her about himself and that, somehow, he was going to help her and his father. He wasn't sure how. He knew that he would get no wages until he was promoted to foot operator, but he would find a way. He had to.

"Sano says the daimyo has raised the price on Saburo's head." Why did she interrupt his thoughts with that statement?

"Who would betray Saburo? He is the only friend the poor have these days."

"That shows how far you have removed yourself from the poor." She was mending the sleeve of her torn kimono. "There is no honor among the hungry. If I knew his name, I would turn him in, in a minute. Ten Saburos are not worth one day of your father's life—or my own, when I am hungry enough. The authorities know this." She bit the thread. "They can wait a little longer—until someone who knows is hungry enough or greedy enough to come forward. They'll come"—she nodded her head knowingly—"Don't worry. Someone will claim that reward. Before this year's rice is harvested. I'd wager my clothes on it."

It was getting dark. He could spend the night, of course. That had been his original idea, but Isako didn't speak of it, and he felt oddly unwelcome. It would be better anyhow, he reasoned, to go back tonight and leave the food with her. He would be fed at the Hanaza, and it would be a waste for him to eat from the little supply that he had brought. He made a pot of tea and served her a cup.

"You must forgive my rudeness, but I must be getting back."

"Oh?" If she had asked him to stay, he would have, but "Oh?" was all she said.

Jiro's tunic was still damp, but he changed into it anyway. He did not want Isako to think that he would impose on her in any way—even to the extent of borrowing one of Hanji's worn-out shirts. He wrapped his sash around his clammy torso and then put on his padded vest.

"Well"—he smiled—"I guess I'm ready." He paused. The words were in his mouth, those words a person uses when he leaves home briefly. "I go only to return," he said softly.

She jerked her head in a bow, but her mouth was set in a straight line, and her eyes revealed nothing. "Hurry back," she said at last.

The cold attacked him like an angry dog, biting at his

face, his hands, his toes and ankles. He pulled his hands up into the sleeves of his tunic and lowered his head into the wind. It was not such a long way—a half hour and he should be back at the Hanaza. He broke into a little trot, but when he did a nose poked out of an alley, so he slowed his steps. He turned his head slightly and tried to look over his shoulder. No one seemed to be following him. Surely he had nothing on him anyone would want to steal, except his vest perhaps. He hugged it to him with his upper arms.

"Oh, forgive me." He had nearly tripped over someone, lying right out in the narrow street. Jiro knelt over the form and distinguished the sparse beard and wrinkled features of an old man. His eyes were open.

"Grandfather? You'll be hurt lying here. Let me help you to the doorway up ahead." He shook the old man gently. "Grandfather?" The frozen eyes stared up into his face. A tiny thrill of fear went through Jiro's body. The poor creature was dead—starved or frozen. Perhaps both. At least he could drag him out of the way, where the body would not be stepped on or rolled over by a cart. Jiro grasped the old man by the shoulders and began to pull him along backward down the street. He'd take the corpse to the next alleyway where, as he told himself, the old man's relatives could find it in the morning and give it a proper burial. Surely someone would come to look for him. He would have a son or a daughter who cared. Jiro saw his own father lying in a street being kicked and stepped on—eaten by hungry dogs. He shuddered. No. He would take care of his father—and his mother. Nothing would happen to them.

"Stop, you little thief." The voice behind him was low. Jiro turned to see a large man with a samurai hairstyle and a long sword raised—one of the ronin that plagued the city like rats. "This street is my territory."

"I-I-I'm not a thief," Jiro protested. "The old man is dead. I was just . . ." He let go of the body and tried to back away, but the ronin grabbed his vest.

"Just taking him to the alley so you could strip him of anything worth having."

"No, really."

"This is *my* territory, you dirty little vulture." He raised his sword higher.

The scene was being played out like a puppet show. If anything, it seemed less real than that to Jiro. How could he be killed by an outlaw samurai on the first night of the New Year? His tunic still smelled faintly of lucky soup and his ears burned with frostbite. An old man might die but not he—his life had hardly begun. If only he had the money, then he could have bribed the ronin. But now, unless he could wrench away from this iron fist . . . .

Then suddenly a *crack*, and the ronin fell at his feet.

"What are you doing out here?" It was the fierce, well-known voice of Yoshida.

"I—"

"You nearly got yourself killed."

"Yes." The boy began to shake—the fright had caught up with him. "Thank you, sir." His teeth were chattering.

"Don't thank me," he said. "You never saw me tonight. Don't forget."

"No sir."

"Now get back as fast as you can."

Jiro bolted like a rabbit from the mouth of a wolf who races to its hole without once looking back.

SEVEN

Okada's New Play

Jiro leaned against the side door of the Hanaza, gasping for breath. He must try to pull himself together before anyone saw him. What a strange and disturbing day—and as the first day of the New Year what did it mean for the year ahead? *Ara!* The thought hit his chest like a snowball. He had forgotten, completely forgotten, to make his New Year pilgrimage. He should have dropped by the shrine at the end of Dotombori this morning on the way to his house, but he'd been so intent on the leaking jug and his anxiety over meeting his mother that it had never entered his head. Jiro would never have prayed from one year to the next, left on his own, but in the past his parents had always got him to a shrine on the first day of the year. Now he had his lack of piety to add to the other troublesome omens of the day. He thought briefly of retracing his steps, but at the moment the prospect of meeting Yoshida along the way was more fearsome than bad luck in the coming year.

"I'm back now," he called at the side door. He was forced to call again twice before he heard a scuffling in the hallway, and at last with the sound of giggles and playful punching, the bolt was drawn, and the door pulled inward to let him enter.

"Ahh, Jiro. Welcome back." Minoru wiped his nose across the back of his sleeve.

"You-you-you missed all the fun." Teiji gave Minoru a punch, and they both began to giggle again.

"You boys drink all the sweet wine between you?" Jiro asked.

"Not quite," Minoru replied cheerfully. "But we tried, right, Teiji?"

"S-s-s-speak for yourself, piglet," Teiji answered and took off down the hallway toward the boys' room with Minoru in clumsy pursuit.

Jiro closed and rebolted the door. It was obvious that Yoshida had not been around lately.

"Yes," Kinshi confirmed later. "Still sick."

"With a little luck"—though drunk, Wada was still cautious enough to look carefully at Kinshi as he spoke— "with a little luck it may last through the holidays."

"With a little luck," Kinshi said, "it may prove fatal." He threw back his head and roared.

Everyone screamed with laughter—except Jiro. The shock he felt at his friend's flaunting disrespect showed plainly on his face. Or perhaps it was the fact that not an hour before Yoshida had saved his life.

Kinshi reached over and rumpled Jiro's hair. "Minoru," he said, "get this lizard face a drink of wine before he spoils our party."

Yoshida didn't set foot in the Hanaza for the first three days of the New Year, but on the fourth he arrived, fully recovered, with a new sign for the notice board. The boys waited impatiently as their elders pressed forward to read the master's amended instructions for Okada's play.

"No," groaned Kinshi softly, who being taller could look over the heads of his elders and see the notice before the other boys. "Why does he do it?"

The play was to open in a week, but Yoshida had

decided at this late date to shift the manipulators around. He himself would remain as chief operator for the bandit Joman—the leading character—but instead of Mochida on the left hand and Kawada on the feet, Mochida was to be chief operator for Fusamu, a courtesan who helped the bandit escape from the authorities. It was technically a small role—the puppet was seen in only one act—but during the time she was on the stage, she laughed and wept, even danced—an operator's dream role. Or nightmare—for there, under the names of Mochida as chief operator and Ueno, one of the senior foot operators, as left-hand operator, Jiro saw his own name. He was to be the foot operator for the character Fusamu. He wasn't ready for such a responsibility. He knew he wasn't. Was that why Kinshi was groaning?

"Look," said Kinshi as if in reply. "Look at that." His finger was on his own name. Kinshi was to be foot operator for the bandit Joman. Kawada was to act as left-hand operator. The elder boy's head was in his hands. "Yoshida knows I can't work with him. Why does he do this?"

"I think his fever affected his brain," Wada said in a hoarse whisper. "Look who he has as foot operator for Fusamu."

"Hey," said Kinshi. "Pull your horns of jealousy back in, Wada. You don't like to do women, anyhow. That's good, Jiro. Yoshida's giving you a big chance."

"I'm not ready."

"Oh, by the time Wada and I finish with you, you'll be ready, won't he, Wada?"

"Yes," said Wada grumpily.

Kinshi gave Wada a friendly punch. "Cheer up. It's more fun to be head boy than bottom foot operator, you know. Anyhow you'll get a chance soon enough."

Wada shrugged. With the capricious Yoshida, one never knew.

To be foot operator for a female puppet has certain difficulties, the first being the fact that the puppet has no feet. Jiro, of course, by now knew how to pinch the inside of the kimono hem with his index and middle fingers to give the illusion of feet and where to place his balled-up fists to resemble the doll's knees when she was kneeling. But dancing! The very word sent terror through his skull. Dancing with all those delicate mincing steps, those turns, coordinating everything perfectly with the head and hands. Sick with apprehension, he almost gave up eating. Instead, while the others ate, he manipulated the "feet" of his lady who hung from the rafters (not the real Fusamu, but an old doll Kinshi had brought him from the storehouse). The others screamed criticisms at him—usually with their mouths full—so his natural anxieties were compounded by his inability to understand half they said.

Jiro left the lamp burning long after the others were in their quilts and practiced before the mirror. Minoru's happy snoring was his only accompaniment, though the next day the fat boy complained bitterly about the light having kept him awake all night.

In the mornings Jiro practiced with Mochida and Ueno. At first, Ueno did not attempt to hide his vexation with Jiro's inexperience. The boy once overheard the operator speak of "the mewling infant Yoshida has strapped to my back." But Mochida, as chief operator, though stern in manner, never beat Jiro or kicked him with his high clogs. Jiro was lucky. Poor Kinshi's right leg was black and blue from Yoshida's kicks.

The days and nights passed in a kind of haze of practice and fear, until quite without warning on the day before dress rehearsals were to begin, Jiro realized that he was no longer struggling to keep up with the men. Fusamu's feet were flowing with the rest of her body. The puppet courtesan was dancing.

At the end of the practice, Mochida and Ueno

nodded at him. They did not praise him or even speak to him about it. That was not the way at the Hanaza. But they did nod at him, which made Jiro know that they, too, felt that Fusamu had come to life at last. They were ready for dress rehearsals with the rest of the cast. Okada, as senior reciter, never practiced, but one of his assistants, Toyotake, chanted the text for the scene with young Tozo accompanying him on the samisen.

The scene told of Joman the bandit seeking refuge in the house of a courtesan named Fusamu. The woman soon falls in love with the rogue and promises to hide him from the pursuing police.

When the authorities arrive, Fusamu allows them to search her house. They find no bandit, just Fusamu's maid and her old bald "mother," who according to the courtesan has come up from the country for a visit, but has fallen ill. Joman, with much coughing and spitting, gives a convincing portrait of a sick old woman.

The police seem satisfied, but just to be sure they set a twenty-four–hour watch around the courtesan's house.

Fusamu begins shrieking and weeping. When the neighbors rush in accompanied by the agents who have been watching the house, she explains that her old mother has died and sends someone to fetch her "country kin" (who are in fact Joman's lieutenants) to carry the body to the burial grounds. For the benefit of the agents, Fusamu apparently goes mad with grief and begins to dance—at first sedately but gradually becoming more and more wild. It takes all three agents to subdue her, and while they are holding her to keep her from harming herself, the "country kin" carry out the "body."

The dance sequence was the crucial one in the scene. Jiro had to stamp his own feet to make the sound of the courtesan's mad steps upon the floor. The voice of Toyotake, the reciter, rose toward this climax, and as it did so, under Jiro's black hood, the sweat broke out on his forehead. But the panic of a week before was gone. He could feel the presence of Mochida and Ueno on either side of him, their bodies tense like wrestlers, their feelings flowing like his into the doll. There were none of the poisons of resentment or anxiety shooting between the three operators now. The trust, the oneness, was taken for granted, and complete attention could be riveted on the doll.

When the scene was over—Joman having been carried out by his cohorts to the shrieks of insane mourning that Toyotake put into Fusamu's mouth—the three of them hurried Fusamu off the stage. Mochida jostled him as if by accident, but Jiro knew it was the operator's way of thanking him. They had performed well for Yoshida. All three of them knew it. And Yoshida was the only audience they feared. *If only my mother could see her clumsy son now*, thought Jiro.

Later, at supper over rice and dried fish, Kinshi spoke to him. "Fusamu breathed today."

"Do you think so?" Jiro tried to keep the excitement out of his voice.

"I can't teach you anything more, you know." Kinshi avoided Jiro's gaze by adding pickles to his rice and carefully emptying his teacup over it. "It would be like a sparrow taking flying lessons from a tortoise." He slurped his rice-and-tea mixture noisily.

"That's nonsense."

"Is it?"

Kinshi turned his eyes toward Jiro. They were full of pain.

It was Jiro's turn to devote himself to noisy eating.

The merchants' purses were full after the New Year, since the poor were duty-bound to pay off all their debts before the turn of the year. And they came in force to the opening of Okada's new play. Word had spread even among the elite that Okada had produced something worth seeing, so the high-level samurai, whose code forbade their indulging in anything so vulgar as the theater, donned their large woven hats for disguise and tried to melt inconspicuously into the crowd sitting on the mat floor of the Hanaza.

The mad dance proved one of the most popular scenes, and Jiro's blood warmed to the shouts and applause from the crowd. Not even the ending dampened the merchants' and warriors' enthusiasm. Jiro had wondered how they would respond to the clever Joman, who did, in uncomfortable ways, resemble Saburo.

Yet these very men who swore publicly that they would put an end to "that devil Saburo" or die in the attempt, these same men held their fat bellies and guffawed to see Joman wriggle his neck from under the ax and make a laughingstock of his pursuers. Straw hats tumbled off the backs of their heads as samurai slapped their thighs and cried to the puppet: "Banzai! Live ten thousand years!"

The authorities were less amused. Every performance was well attended by known spies and undercover agents. "But," as Kinshi pointed out, "they all pay at the door." So as a result of the combined popularity and notoriety of the play, the Hanaza was doing the best business in town.

EIGHT

Command Performance

February thawed into March, and March after a show of fickleness warmed into April. At the Hanaza *The Thief of the Tokaido* continued to bloom with money and acclaim through the change of season. Fusamu got thundering applause night after night. Kinshi's bruised right leg was beginning to return to its normal color. All in all the theater was almost a cheerful place during that spring.

Outside the walls of the theater, the city was greeting the new season in quite a different mood. Perhaps the cold had frozen the poor into inaction during the winter, for now bands of desperate men and women, sometimes with children in tow, roamed the streets. The spring nights were alive with these night rovers. They may have had some destination in mind or some aim—no one dared ask. Occasionally one of these bands would let loose a barrage of stones against the night shutters of a shop or the gates of a wealthy man's house, but mostly they seemed to wander the earth like spirits refused entrance to either heaven or hell.

One night Jiro awoke to hear pounding on the alley door. His first thought was that it was night rovers, and though, as junior boy it was his duty to answer the door at night, he curled farther under his quilt and tried to shut out the noise.

"Jiro!" Kinshi's voice came across the darkness. "There's someone at the door. Wake up!"

"I'm awake. It's night rovers, don't you think?"

"No, too persistent. I'll go with you."

The two boys passed down the dark hallway. Now there was a voice added to the pounding.

"We're coming!" Kinshi yelled, waking up the rest of the west side of the Hanaza that had not already been awakened by the visitor.

"Be careful," Jiro said as the older boy slid back the bolt and opened the door a crack. Kinshi put one eye at the crack.

"Who is it?"

Jiro stood close to Kinshi against the door in case they should need to slam it shut. "Who's there?" he whispered.

"No one," Kinshi said. "He must have gone." He pulled open the door a little wider and stuck his head into the alley. Jiro nudged until he could peer out as well. There was no one in sight. The visitor must have run when Kinshi called out.

"What's this?" Kinshi twisted about. A white paper was nailed to the door. He tore it off the nail.

The boys rebolted the door. "We've got to get a light, Jiro. It's a message of some kind."

Mochida was in the hall outside his room. "What's all the commotion?" he asked.

Kinshi held out the paper. "Someone left this on the door and ran away."

"Come on in here." He took the boys into the room that he shared with three other operators, all of whom were propped up on their quilts. Mochida got the fire stones and struck them to light a lamp. "Now let's see what mischief this is."

It was a beautifully brush-stroked notice, as carefully done as a formal poem. And it read:

> *The King of Thieves (known by some as Saburo) will be at the Hanaza on Thursday for a command performance of the play,* The Thief of the Tokaido, *to begin at dusk. Admission to this performance is to be free to as many of his loyal subjects—the poor of Osaka—as can enter the theater. Until then . . . .*

"Saburo!" Kinshi was obviously delighted. "Saburo in our theater!"

"Yes," said Mochida. "We were about ripe for a disaster. Things have gone far too well lately." He looked at the boys. "I suppose it is my fate to carry this message of doom to Yoshida?" Neither the boys nor his fellow operators volunteered to relieve him. But Mochida later reported that Yoshida had received the news with remarkable serenity and ordered that the notice be posted in the courtyard.

Jiro's reaction to the notice was more like Mochida's than Kinshi's. He studied the words as though they were some kind of warning to him. But it was as if the warning was written in a foreign tongue, so he did not know how to obey it.

For the others at the Hanaza, the bandit's message was a source of excited speculation. They gathered in knots before the notice board and argued whether the beautiful brushstrokes meant that the brigand was a scholar or simply that he had access to an accomplished scribe. "But the boldness of the man—just imagine it!" This was the point upon which everyone agreed, including the authorities.

Special agents appeared at the theater in force, demanding to know the meaning of Yoshida's poster. An assistant magistrate came on horseback accompanied by two underassistants, each of whom had brought five of his own assistants, which indicated how seriously the matter was being regarded by the daimyo.

The assistant magistrate rode to the alley entrance and dismounted with ceremony. He wore the two swords of a high-level samurai with a black skirted garment and a black overcloak on the back of which was woven the spread-winged heron crest of his noble family. He did not stop to remove his clogs but stormed into Yoshida's dressing room, his small army behind him.

During the noisy session with Yoshida, every member of the Hanaza who had not been summoned to the meeting found some excuse to work as close as possible to the door. Jiro was carefully sweeping the courtyard for the third time when the assistant magistrate, his men following behind like proud ducklings after a pompous mother, marched into the courtyard. At his order two assistants to the underassistants ripped Saburo's brush-stroked message from the notice board and tore it elaborately to shreds.

No such performance was to be allowed. The poor were already in an ugly mood—simply to allow a crowd of them to gather in a public place was dangerous and to allow it after nightfall was out of the question.

"Yes," Yoshida agreed. "You're quite wise. For my own part, I certainly have no wish to see my theater torn apart by an unruly mob. Still . . ."

"Still what?" the assistant magistrate demanded.

"Still from the point of view of those in authority—to know that Saburo is to be in a certain place at a certain time . . . ." Jiro had to look up from his sweeping to make sure it was Yoshida speaking. He had never heard the tone before. The master puppeteer sounded more like a poor relative at a New Year's feast. His obsequious voice went on. "You, sir, are an unusual man, being able, in this way, to put the good of the city first. I suppose a lesser

man would be tempted—thinking only of his honor—or even of the reward . . ."

"It's a trick, you fool. Saburo would never come. He simply wants the police busy in one place while he works his mischief in another."

"Oh, I see," Yoshida said. "Of course, you're right. He'd never come here. Not even Saburo is that brazen. He's not stupid, after all."

Why, he's playing a part, thought Jiro. *He's trying to manipulate the police officer like . . . .*

But the assistant magistrate had turned his back with the great heron crest on Yoshida in the middle of the puppeteer's speech as if determined to be as rude as possible. A sharp order and he and his little flock of underassistants and their assistants swaggered across the courtyard and out the alley door.

They were back before dark. The daimyo had intervened. The assistant magistrate could hardly conceal his rage as he informed Yoshida that his Lordship had commanded the performance to take place.

"But my theater!" The master puppeteer's voice almost squeaked. "You yourself said this very morning that . . . ."

"I do as I am ordered, puppeteer," said the assistant magistrate through his teeth. "And so will you." At the gate he turned again. "There will be plenty of police here, never fear. Plenty of police."

An ordinary performance at the Hanaza began in the morning and ran until dusk, to take full advantage of the daylight hours. But Saburo had specified that the performance should begin at dusk, and no one considered that he was the sort of fellow who would accept a compromise. Every lamp in the theater was brought. Then Yoshida sent the married men to their houses to gather any that were available there. Even the musicians in the east wing were called upon to contribute their lamps, and the boys were set to work inserting pegs along the wall and in the pillars from which lamps could be hung. There was to be a row of lamps across the top of the apron that enclosed the stage area. Everyone was frantic with preparation and anticipation except Mochida, who was frantic with fear that someone would stumble into a lamp and transform the glory of the Hanaza into charcoal for a ragpicker's soup.

By dusk on Thursday there were more than the one hundred people that the theater could accommodate waiting outside the entrance. The police were let in first. About ten of them, including the assistant magistrate, they arranged themselves at strategic points throughout the theater. Then the theater was filled with the smell of unwashed bodies and the nervous twitchings of men, women, and children who have nothing but anger upon which to feed. More police were set outside the front entrance and the west and east alley entrances to the dressing-room areas.

Kinshi and Jiro stood in the wings and looked over the audience of police and paupers. It was as though a fisherman had thrown out his net without looking and hauled in a catch of stinging nettles along with a few shiny carp and a fat octopus or two.

"Look." Jiro jabbed Kinshi. "In the middle toward the left side."

Kinshi tried to follow the direction of Jiro's nodding head. "Where?"

"The small woman in gray. It's my mother." Suddenly he felt sick. Suppose there was a riot in the theater tonight. "Kinshi. Please. Go down and tell her to leave. She wouldn't listen to me."

"Let her be. When will she ever have another chance to see her son perform? It would be too bad for her to miss your Fusamu."

"Where's *your* mother tonight?"

"At home. Yoshida had some jobs—"

"You see. Yoshida doesn't want her around tonight. He knows there's likely to be trouble." What else did Yoshida know? Jiro could not get the act before the police officer out of his mind. "Persuade my mother to go home, please."

"Nonsense. I'll go down and tell her to watch Fusamu's feet." Kinshi went to the front of the stage area and unceremoniously descended, swinging one long leg at a time over the apron. The people packed into the front row shifted slightly as he brought his big feet down among them and stepped over and around them, making his way to the place where Isako sat on the matting. There was no place for Kinshi to kneel, so he bent over her like a large bird, his hands resting on his knees with his elbows flopping as he talked. Isako was jerking her head in nervous little bows and nods that completed the picture of a sparrow who finds itself confronted by a friendly stork and is not quite sure what to do. At length, Kinshi bowed deeply, his head nearly hitting the small woman's as he did so, and picked his way back through the crowd bobbing apologies left and right since his feet were too big ever to choose a spot that had not already been claimed.

"What did she say?"

"What do mothers always say?" Kinshi said. "The usual sweet bean paste. How proud she is . . . ."

"My mother doesn't talk like that."

"Actually," Kinshi said, "she didn't say a word. I just thought you'd feel better if I . . ." He finished lamely with a shrug.

"Did you tell her to leave?"

"No, of course not. I told her not to miss the third act."

There was nothing to be done. It was time for the performance to begin. Kinshi went to the dressing room to put on his hood for the first act. Teiji came to take his position at the curtain.

"W-w-which one do you think is Saburo?" he whispered.

"Saburo?"

"H-h-he's out there somewhere." Teiji studied the audience face by face. "H-h-how about that dirty-faced ronin on the front row? No. T-t-too obvious." He giggled. "More l-l-likely to be one of the policemen or even"—he punched Jiro and pointed with his nose—"that funny-looking little woman on the left with the fierce face."

"That's my mother."

"Oh, Jiro. I'm s-s-sorry." Poor Teiji looked stricken with remorse.

"It's all right. She *is* pretty fierce."

A hooded Wada had come onto the stage from the left wings. He knocked together a pair of wooden blocks and called the audience to attention by reciting the names of performers for *The Thief of the Tokaido*. His voice trailed off with the call: "*Tozai! Tozai-i-i-i! Hear ye! Hear ye!*"

Okada raised the text and bowed his head. The first notes on the samisen were struck. "Once many years ago there lived an extraordinary man . . . ." In the fast fading light of the spring afternoon the command performance had begun.

Never had the Hanaza had such an audience. They shrieked with laughter and clapped their hands together whenever Joman outwitted the dull authorities. They wept openly, man and woman alike, when Joman's young son died rather than reveal his father's whereabouts. And when Fusamu danced her manic dance and the "body" of Joman was carried to safety, they jumped to their feet and stamped the floor. "Banzai!" they screamed. "Banzai!" and Jiro could not help feeling glad that his mother was there to hear the cheering.

When it was close to completely dark in the theater, Jiro and Wada lit the line of lamps across the apron, along the walls, and on the pillars. The police shifted uneasily in their narrow places.

It was in the next scene that Joman discovered that there was a traitor in his band. He designed a series of tests in order to discover the identity of his would-be betrayer. But not even the wily Joman suspected that his own wife was prepared to turn him in to the authorities.

Jiro took over Teiji's curtain duty so that his friend could get ready to handle a one-man soldier puppet. The audience groaned as Joman tested one after the other of his loyal followers while behind him the true villain sat weaving like a proper country wife.

Now and again someone cried out, "Behind you, Joman, behind you," or "It's her. The one who shares your bed." The audience could not have been more involved had they been on the stage themselves. "Joman! Look!" The woman had risen from her loom and set a lantern at the front door of the country home that was Joman's hideout. In the darkness the soldiers crept up to surround the house. They had seen the signal. Everyone but the hapless Joman had seen it. He (O fool to trust a woman!) took a cup of drugged wine from his wife's treacherous hand, and then, feeling sleep stealing upon his limbs, lay down like a babe in the quilts she had spread for him. "No, Joman, no!" the audience cried as the scene ended and their hero appeared hopelessly trapped.

Jiro and Wada moved in to change the scenery. The next setting was that of the small house near the execution grounds where Joman was being kept prisoner. He was due to die the following day. Jiro had to sit out of sight behind the partition and hold a branch with paper cherry blossoms fastened to it.

The thought of a young man or woman dying in the spring was always poignant. Even the street people in tonight's audience sighed when they saw the branch.

Joman's faithless wife appeared. The crowd hissed

between their teeth. She stood under the cherry bough and remembered other springs—when love was young and the world seemed pure and bright. Suddenly she heard a voice from inside the house—it was Joman singing an old ballad about the fickleness of women and the shortness and uncertainty of human life. As she listened, the wretched woman was seized with remorse. She took from her sleeve the tiny dagger a woman always carried for protection, and meditating upon her sins and the unhappiness of fate, she at length plunged the blade deep into her bosom, calling out to Joman, "Forgive me! Forgive me!" as she gracefully died.

Following this scene, the audience debated. Should Joman forgive her—traitor that she was? Never, some declared. To betray one's husband is to bring eternal dishonor upon oneself. But, said others, did she not pay her debt to honor by taking her own life?

The chanter and samisen player appeared for the final act, so all arguments ceased and every eye strained toward the dimly lit stage.

When the soldiers came to take Joman to the execution ground, it was a dark and stormy day. (Backstage Jiro was banging metal pots together while Wada and Teiji at either side of the stage at the rear rippled a long yellow ribbon of silk between them to make the effect of lightning.)

A group of ghostly figures appeared. The soldiers, frightened but determined to carry out their duty, went into the room where Joman was imprisoned to take him out to the burial ground. They found him on the floor apparently lifeless. From above a ghostly voice was heard: "Oh, my brothers, my soul has already departed this worthless flesh and is even now in torment for all my sins." (Howling was added to the lightning crashes backstage.) "Throw out the hull which once housed such poisonous fruit that it may be eaten by the crows. Then get you to the temple to pray that your hands which are contaminated with evil may be cleansed." (More howls and crashes)

The puppet soldiers were shaking visibly, but a sense of duty drove one of them to suggest that they behead the body anyway, since they were supposed to present a head to the daimyo as proof that they have carried out their duty. "Yes," the ghostly voice agreed, "separate this cursed head from my body and hang it on a post outside the city gate. For it has great powers to cleanse this city from all its wickedness." (Louder howls and crashes) "One look at these eyes, and any man who has ever lied will find his mouth covered with terrible sores. Any man who has strayed from his wife by so much as a flirtatious glance will fall deathly ill with plague, and any man who has stolen, or even envied that which belongs to another, his hands will drop off at the wrist. Thus the city will be cleansed not only of every evildoer, but of any whose hearts have been shadowed by evil thoughts. Yes, take my head, you men of great courage. You whose hearts are without any stain."

By this time the soldiers were almost senseless with fear. They decided to behead the body of Joman's wife and take it, wrapped in a kerchief, to the daimyo and repeat the ghostly message in case the old fellow got any ideas about unwrapping the package and having a look.

When they were gone, Joman jumped up, the brigand who had produced the ghostly voice slid off the roof, those who had posed as the ghostly figures came running, and the rogue and his band were reunited with great joy and to the thunderous applause of the audience.

Okada, who had chanted the final act, as well as the first, the third, and the fifth, raised the text and bowed.

Suddenly, as though by signal, everyone near a lamp leaned over and extinguished it. Along with the light, the applauding and cheering stopped just as abruptly as if its wick had been snuffed as well.

Over the silent darkness a voice floated. "Thank you, my friends, both those who performed and those who came to be entertained. When the signal is given, please leave the theater quietly and do not draw attention to yourselves, for there are police on guard outside. The performers are to count slowly to five thousand before they relight the lamps. And remember, my friends, the horror you felt when Joman was betrayed. Remember *that* should any of you ever feel similarly tempted."

The theater was almost silent, waiting for another word from Saburo. At last the voice said, "Now you may go."

Jiro could hear the crowd, shuffling quietly from the theater. He waited motionless in darkness until a low voice said, "Five thousand. We can light the lamps now."

Jiro struck the firestones until a spark caught the wick of the first lamp. Then he moved to the next. As the lamps flickered and flamed one by one, they revealed a strange sight. The assistant magistrate and the other police officers who had marched into the theater with such pomposity a few hours before were standing in their loincloths, their legs bound and their arms raised above their heads with their hands tied together by their thumbs. Over tightly bound gags their eyes flashed, daring anyone to smile.

Yoshida rushed forward to untie the assistant magistrate, who without his heron-crested cloak and his two swords looked pathetically ordinary. "Sir, what a terrible thing. I am mortified that my theater . . . ."

"Send someone out to tell the men on the outside to bring us clothes."

"Kinshi!" Yoshida said, but his voice lacked its usual steel. Kinshi ran outside.

"And Yoshida," the officer continued, "I take it upon

myself to order you not to perform this play again. Do you understand?"

"Oh, yes, sir. Of course we never meant . . ."

"Too much has been construed."

"Yes, sir. That rogue has twisted it to suit his purposes. We will not present it again." Yoshida turned to Jiro, his head bent forward, his voice ingratiating. "You, boy, go bring some wine for the gentlemen here—and some kimonos for them to wear until their clothes arrive."

Jiro did not dare look his master in the eye. He jerked his head in a bow and hurried to obey.

NINE

Night Rovers

Yoshida was in a vile mood. His most profitable production in several years had been shut down by the police, and he had nothing ready with which to replace it. He slapped a notice on the entranceway board declaring the theater indefinitely closed and roamed the courtyard and the dressing rooms screaming at everyone he saw. If a person was idle, he cursed heaven that he had been set upon by an infestation of lice who did nothing but fatten their foul bodies under his hair. If a person was busily engaged, he kicked the broom or sewing from his hands and cursed heaven that he had been inflicted with a hill of ants who went scurrying about making a great appearance of business but who obviously lacked any intelligence or goal.

Jiro, who stood around stupidly after a broom had been kicked from his hands, stared at the master puppeteer and tried to figure out what was going on. Either the man was an unreasonable monster—which was what most people seemed to think—or there was something else. He could not shake the feeling that today's performance was just that—a performance. Yoshida's cruelty was as much of an act as his subservience in his dealings with the police had been. Yoshida met Jiro's staring with a contemptuous glare and marched into the east-wing dressing rooms, yelling to see Okada.

When he came out a few minutes later, he announced to anyone in earshot that the next production would be a repeat of *The Battle of Dannoura*. He would post duties tomorrow, and he expected everyone to be ready to open Sunday. There was not so much wealth at the Hanaza that they could continue to loll about indefinitely, he said, though it was obvious that some were regarding the enforced closing as a second New Year's.

"That gives us exactly one day to prepare!" complained Wada.

"Don't worry," Kinshi said. "He's not going to have you do feet for this play. He's known all over Osaka for the 'Torture by Koto' scene, and he won't risk his reputation on an untried boy."

Wada pushed out his underlip in a pout. "I'm not expecting him to put me on feet for Akoya. Anyhow, I'm not planning to specialize in women puppets."

"You'll get your chance, Wada." Kinshi jabbed the pouting mouth with his knuckles. "'Even the snow on Fuji gets to the sea,' as Mochida would say."

"Mochida is not running this troupe," replied Wada, throwing a dark look in Jiro's direction. Jiro blushed and prayed that no one could read his mind, for he knew in his heart he was more ambitious than any junior boy had a right to be.

The Hanaza heard the story next morning from the fishmonger. A squad of police under an assistant magistrate had presented themselves at the gate of Morikawa the moneylender on the previous night and demanded that he reveal the whereabouts of Saburo. They had proof, the officer said, that the paper on which Saburo's message to the puppet theater had been written had come from Morikawa's shop. Although the moneylender protested his innocence, two policemen led him off kicking and weeping to jail while the others searched the premises. Of course when the magistrate was contacted in the morning, he knew nothing of the affair. Poor Morikawa had spent a most unhappy night with the condemned criminals and bedbugs of Osaka only to return home and learn that the "police" who had searched for evidence had cleaned out his treasure boxes of the better part of his fortune. Only the fact that half the city owed him money, an obligation which, of course, had to be repaid before the next New Year's, prevented his being completely bereft of fortune.

Saburo had obviously put to use the police dress and credentials he and his band had taken at the Hanaza the night before. He had even managed to fool the jailers with his disguise. Now the wealthy were saying that they would never be able to trust another policeman.

Yoshida stormed in while the fishmonger was still telling his tale, which brought the entertainment to a hasty end. The master puppeteer pounded up the new notice and then stalked back to his dressing room, bellowing for tea. As junior boy, it was Jiro's duty to fetch it, so it was not until later that he learned that Yoshida had put Kawada on as left-hand operator for one of the soldiers and that Kinshi was to manipulate Akoya's feet.

Jiro's immediate, unbidden reaction was disappointment. He had nursed a tiny hope that perhaps he would be assigned to do Akoya's feet—but now he was ashamed of it. He pounded Kinshi on the back a little harder than he meant to. "Congratulations, Kinshi. You see, you showed Yoshida last time you could do it."

"Do you think that's it?" All Kinshi's self-confidence oozed away when confronted with some unfathomable action of his father's.

"Of course. He stopped kicking you, right?"

"Not immediately."

"No, but as you relaxed and started working well with him, he did."

Kinshi was nervously pulling at his nose. "But that was a male role. I'm not as good with women."

"Of course you are. You never give yourself proper credit."

Kinshi grinned. "You're beginning to sound like me."

"Am I?"

"Thanks, Jiro. I'll go get a doll from the storehouse and practice." Kinshi started toward the storehouse with Jiro beside him. Halfway across the courtyard Jiro hesitated. The storehouse was off limits for the boys, though Kinshi often went in to "borrow" puppets for practice. "Oh, come on," the older boy said. "How can it hurt if you come inside just this once?"

Unlike the rest of the buildings which comprised the Hanaza, the storehouse was not built of wood. Its thick walls were a mixture of mud and plaster, which made it virtually fireproof. There was a pair of great iron doors on the west side that were fastened open so that air could pass through the iron grating of the inner sliding door into the dark interior of the building. One tiny window above the door let a splinter of light into the upper floor.

Kinshi reached up and took a key from the top of the door frame and unlocked the iron-grating door, sliding it open wide enough for the boys to slip in and closing it after them. There were others in the courtyard, but everyone was careful not to watch the boys' surreptitious entrance. Jiro was beginning to understand. All of the Hanaza was a play—not just what they did upon the stage, but off it as well. Each person had a part—that was why when someone like himself didn't know the lines, he could disturb the whole drama. He had done that when he had insisted on getting the script for the new play. That was Kinshi's role, and he had usurped it. He must be more careful. The last person in the world that he wanted to offend was Kinshi.

From the doorway Jiro could see to his left shelves lined with puppet heads, which faded into shadowy blobs a few steps from the entrance. On the right were stage props, and hanging from the ceiling were seven or eight fully assembled dolls. Kinshi pushed over a chest and climbed up to unfasten one of the female puppets.

"It's a wonder they don't mildew in here," said Jiro. Despite the precaution of the open door, the storehouse felt clammy.

"Oh, they do." Kinshi shoved the doll he had gotten down under Jiro's nose. "Don't worry. Yoshida wouldn't leave a costume of any worth in here. These old things aren't good for anything except for us to practice on. Apprentices are not supposed to notice the stink."

Jiro wandered a little farther into the dark belly of the room. "There's a lot of stuff in here. What's it all for?"

"Who knows? Yoshida never throws away anything."

Jiro's eyes were gradually adjusting to the dim light. There at the back was a staircase leading to the upper floor. "What's up there?"

"The second floor." Kinshi's voice was impatient.

"Yes." Jiro hesitated, one foot on the bottom stair.

"We're not supposed to be in here at all, you know."

"Yes, all right." Reluctantly Jiro followed the older boy out of the storehouse and out into the courtyard, where they stood for a moment blinking in the bright spring sunshine. He had almost missed his line in the play again. He must be more careful.

With only one day to prepare there was no time for Jiro to sit about and watch his friend practice. But as he worked with the other boys to mend and repaint the old sets, his mind was always in the dressing room with Kinshi.

He wanted his friend to do well. Of course, that was what he wanted more than anything in the whole world. But Kinshi didn't really want to do the female roles—Kinshi didn't even feel that he was good with women puppets, whereas Jiro . . . . He tried to stuff disloyal thoughts back, deep into the darkness within himself. He did, he swore to himself, want more than anything else, more than anything in the whole world, for Kinshi to prove to Yoshida his skill and worth as a puppeteer. There would be other times for Jiro to perform. He was the most junior of all the boys; it wouldn't be fair for Yoshida to advance him more quickly—and yet—there it was—ambition—wriggling back up to the surface like an earthworm after rain.

And when at supper he asked Kinshi in all sincerity, "How is it going?" and Kinshi replied through clenched teeth, "Terrible," Jiro felt a tiny leap of pleasure in his traitorous bosom.

He clenched his own teeth. "You can do it." But he must have sounded strange because Kinshi gave him a puzzled look before he nodded his thanks for Jiro's encouragement.

After supper Kinshi went to practice with Yoshida and Kawada. Jiro and the other boys were in their dressing room. Mochida had given them the excruciatingly tiresome job of ripping apart all the costumes that had been used for *The Thief of the Tokaido*. After each garment had been taken apart, the pieces were carefully washed and flattened out to dry, and then the whole thing had to be sewn together again. Jiro had had his fill of costume making and remaking when he had been at home. Now bent over this irksome task, the voice of Isako seemed to be constantly in his ear, screaming at him to be careful— No! too late—See what you did!—Stupid boy!—You'll ruin everything. With every tiny stitch he snipped, his nerves grew more raw until he felt like a turnip on a grater.

"Oh, the devil take it," he muttered. "How can

anyone see to cut these tedious little stitches at this time
of night?"

Wada looked over at him. "Perhaps if the rest of us
applauded, you'd find the task more to your liking."

"Oh, be quiet, Wada."

Wada rose to his feet. "What do you mean telling
me to be quiet? You can't seem to remember, Jiro, that I
am your senior."

"I'm sorry," Jiro mumbled. "I didn't mean to offend
you."

"S-s-sit down, Wada," Teiji said gently. "Can't you
see? H-h-he's worried about Kinshi"—Teiji jabbed his
head in the direction of the theater—"i-i-in there."

They all sat quietly and concentrated on the sounds
coming down the hall. All they could hear was a voice
chanting the scene, "Torture by Koto." They strained to
hear grunts or shouts—indications of Yoshida's anger—
but there were none. The practice seemed to be going
smoothly.

"S-s-see, you can relax, Jiro. Kinshi's doing all right."

Jiro attempted a smile. Teiji's childlike face was so
open, his own concern for Kinshi so pure, so unpolluted
with selfishness or ambition. Jiro nodded and jerked his
head down closely over his work. He did not want Teiji to
read his expression and find something unworthy there.

"What's that?" All the boys jumped to their feet at
the sound.

"Stones," said Jiro. "Probably night rovers throwing
stones at the building." He turned to Wada. "What
should we do?"

"What should we do?" Wada yelled over the shower
of rocks. "How should I know? Kinshi's up there near the
door. And Yoshida. They're both right there."

"But you're senior boy here."

Wada looked closely into Jiro's eyes. "Are you trying
to make fun of me?"

"No. Would you like for me to go to the door and see what's happening?"

The building rattled under another assault of stones. "Yes," Wada said tightly. "Tell them to go away."

Going down the dark hall, Jiro didn't feel nearly as brave as he had in front of Wada, so he was grateful that Teiji followed him out of the room. From the theater the chanting was proceeding as though nothing else mattered.

"I'll just open it a crack. Stay close by, Teiji, in case we have to slam it shut fast."

Jiro lifted the bolt as quietly as he could and opened the door just enough to allow himself a one-eyed view of the alley. It was filled with people. Some of them were carrying torches.

"All right, once more," a voice came out of the crowd. "Make him hear us this time." The mob let loose rocks, some of which struck the wooden walls with force and bounced back into the crowd. There were shouts and complaints from those who were hit.

"Shut up," commanded the leader's voice. "All together now. Call Yoshida."

"Hey," someone said, "the door's open." Everyone turned and began pushing toward the door. Jiro and Teiji slammed it shut and threw the bolt. They leaned against it, the narrow escape taking their breath like a long run.

"What do we do n-n-now?"

"I don't know, you're my senior."

"Oh, Jiro," Teiji's voice came out like a laugh. "M-m-me?"

The night rovers were banging on the door. There were shouts of "Yoshida! Yoshida!"

"M-m-maybe we'd b-b-better call Yoshida."

From backstage they could hear the chanting continuing, though it was nearly drowned out by the noise outside. The boys hesitated.

Jiro swallowed. "Do you want me to tell him?"

"Oh, would you? H-h-he hates the way I stutter."

Jiro moved to the curtain and stood against the wall, from which he could see the scene. If any of the puppeteers noticed him, they pretended not to. None of them was wearing a hood, but Yoshida's eyes veiled the expression on his face. Jiro could not really see Kinshi, for he was blocked by his puppet as he bent over on the other side of Yoshida, who, standing on foot-high clogs, towered over his assistants. The puppet Akoya was playing the koto. A chill went through Jiro's body. Yoshida was really a master—all of them were. The first time he had stood and watched this scene, he had thought it magnificent, but as a child judges something he cannot understand. Now he knew; now his blood raced to his arm, and he could feel his own fingers and wrist moving with those of the puppeteers. Mentally, he shifted positions—from Yoshida to Mochida on the left and then to Kinshi—motionless, holding the knees of the puppet just so for the duration of the tense concert. Kinshi was doing well. He could feel that from the utter trust with which Yoshida and Mochida were making their own movements. *I'm glad,* Jiro told himself. *He deserves this. My time will come.* He tried to comfort himself.

The noise outside the alley door was mounting. Teiji was suddenly there beside him. "Th-th-they may knock down the door."

Jiro held up his hand. He shook his head. Better the door down than this scene needlessly interrupted.

During the remainder of the scene the chanting and samisen were nearly drowned out by the cries and banging from the alley. Those on stage proceeded with utter concentration. They drew Jiro into their magic circle. He would have been able utterly to dismiss the night rovers if it had not been for Teiji running back and forth distractedly between the stage and the alley door like a goldfish who has spied a cat on either side of his small pond.

After the last note of the samisen died away, the puppeteers held their position for a few seconds and then relaxed. At that moment Teiji ran out onto the stage.

"M-m-m-master." The stuttering so overcame him that he simply nodded his head toward the alley door where the shouts of "Yoshida!" and the pounding seemed to have increased in volume and ferocity since the scene ended.

"Who are they?" Yoshida snapped.

Teiji's body tensed. The veins on his neck protruded. "N-n-n-n—" He fought for the word that would not come.

"Night rovers." Jiro jumped in.

Yoshida turned to him. "So? And what do they want with me?"

"I don't know, sir." Jiro lowered his eyes. "We didn't ask. We thought we ought to speak to you first."

"Well, go ask them," Yoshida yelled.

Jiro raced for the door with Teiji at his heels. Teiji nodded his head as if to say, "You talk. You know I can't." So without opening the door Jiro yelled at the top of his voice: "Yoshida wants to know your business with him."

The pounding and shouting stopped abruptly. The voice that Jiro recognized earlier as belonging to the leader replied: "We want food. Tell Yoshida to give us rice, and we'll go away."

The boys ran back to the stage. "They want rice, sir."

"I heard them." Yoshida was putting the miniature instruments used by the puppet into their quilted covers and giving them to Mochida and Kinshi to put away. Jiro waited for him to say something more, but he didn't.

"Well, sir?"

"Well, what?" Yoshida turned toward Jiro impatiently.

"Well—" Now he understood why Teiji stammered. "Well, what do you want me to say to them?"

"Nothing."

"Nothing?"

"Nothing!" Yoshida roared the word into his face. Jiro stepped backward, nearly knocking Teiji to the floor. "Do you think I'll let a bunch of thieving beggars bully me?"

"They're hungry, Yoshida." Kinshi spoke quietly, but there was no fear in his voice. "We have enough. Why don't you give them a little?"

Yoshida swirled around, stamping his high clogs on the wooden floor. "You sentimental little fool! What do you suppose would happen if I gave rice tonight to a mob of hoodlums who banged upon my door? Where would be the end of it? The whole city—the whole country is hungry." He turned back to Jiro and Teiji. "Get the mallets from the kitchen—the ones we beat the New Year's rice with. If anyone breaks into this door, you be here to see they don't get any farther."

Kinshi opened his mouth as if to speak, but Yoshida pushed Jiro aside and marched past him to his dressing room.

"Go to bed, Kinshi," Mochida spoke for the first time. "The boys here can take care of things."

Kinshi hesitated.

"G-g-go on. Y-y-you have to go on stage tomorrow. F-f-fetch the mallets, Jiro."

The two of them sat out the night in front of the door, mallets in hand. As the night wore on, Jiro grew cold and his stomach felt queasy from lack of sleep. The night rovers kept up their disturbance, but the door was a strong one, and though there were anxious moments when it seemed that nothing could withstand the hammering and battering, the thick pine held and did not give way.

By dawn Jiro was nearly ill with listening and waiting. He hated everyone: the night rovers for taking away his sleep; Yoshida for refusing to speak to them; Kinshi for having pity on brutes like these; even poor Teiji, who sat opposite him, quiet and uncomplaining.

Down the hallway they could hear someone—Mochida probably—shoving open his night shutters. It must be nearly morning. Jiro stood up and nearly fell. His legs had gone to sleep under him. What a terrible night, but at least it was nearly over. The pounding had ceased and the night rovers were talking among themselves. Now and again a voice would call an insult from a distance down the alley. They must be dispersing. Jiro nodded at Teiji. Teiji got up and stretched and yawned. It was nearly over.

Suddenly a harsh female voice cut through the low rumble at the mouth of the alley. "Yoshida! May you spend eternity as foot manipulator for the devil!" The curse was greeted with a chorus of raucous laughter.

Jiro leaned heavily against the door. Isako. But what was she doing out there with *them*? Should he open the door and try to slip out to her before the night rovers saw the crack and plunged through it?

Teiji was staring at him.

He could no longer hear their voices now. The night rovers had all left the alley. Isako would be going home. Surely she would already be well down Dotombori by this time. Besides, what would he do if he caught up with her? He had nothing to give her. Jiro looked down at the mallet which had been in his hand all night. What if—suppose the night rovers had managed to break the door, might he have struck her down?

For a moment he thought he was going to be sick, but the nausea passed.

"I-i-it's morning," said Teiji. "Let's make the f-f-f-fires."

"Yes," said Jiro. "Yes. Let's go."

TEN

Anxieties

Jiro felt ill all that day. He got down a few swallows of his breakfast soup but was so afraid that it was coming right back up that he rushed from the dressing room into the courtyard.

"What's the matter?" Kinshi had followed him out.

"Nothing. My stomach. I didn't get any sleep last night."

"I'll ask my mother to make you some rice gruel. That might help settle your belly."

"No, it's all right. I don't want anything."

Kinshi nodded. "I knew you'd feel the way I do."

"What do you mean?"

"That it's wrong—criminal—for us to have food and refuse to share it with those poor starving wretches."

"So you . . . ."

"Do you know what I'd really like to do?"

"What?"

"I'd like to join Saburo. The only problem is that those raids of his make a great show, but they don't really accomplish anything—like shooting a quiver of arrows at the ocean. If I were one of his men, I'd convince him to organize the night rovers, all the hungry people of the city into a kind of army. You could plan your battle strategy . . . ." Kinshi looked up. "Of course there's another problem."

"What?"

Kinshi shrugged. "I wouldn't know where to start looking for Saburo."

"No," said Jiro, his stomach churning more than before. "Perhaps I should try some of the gruel."

"Oh, sure. Go back and lie down. You can rest a few minutes before you have to start cleaning up the breakfast things. I'll hurry."

By the time the gruel was ready, Jiro was hard at work sweeping up the stage. Kinshi gave him the bowl with his chopsticks, smiling apologetically at the delay. Jiro gulped down his breakfast where he stood. He felt dizzy from hunger as well as from lack of sleep, and the bland gruel slid down easily. Kinshi was kind. Stubborn and unwise, but always kind. What would have happened if Kinshi had been left to guard the door last night? He would probably have let those cutthroats right in. Jiro had a mental picture of the night rovers crawling all over the Hanaza grounds like ants over a dead slug. For once Yoshida had been right. There is no way to help people once they've turned the corner toward beastliness. One can only protect oneself. In his mind he raised his rice mallet to smash the whole stinking crowd, when one of them turned and looked him full in the face. *Oh, Mother, I didn't mean you. Go home,* he pleaded. *And stay there. I'll find some way to help you. I swear it. I will.* He began to sweep furiously, while huge tears sprang to his eyes and splashed down his face.

The first performance of *The Battle of Dannoura* was a success, though Jiro was not aware of it. He watched the stage as though from the inside of a waterfall. He could barely see what was going on, and he did his backstage duties as though there was great pressure beating down against every limb. There was even a roaring in his ears that nearly drowned out the chanting.

Afterward he fell into his quilt without bothering to undress. He was vaguely aware that Kinshi was trying to talk to him, but he couldn't make the effort to listen. So he just mumbled, "You did well, very-well-well . . . ," and turned his face to the wall.

He awoke with a start. It couldn't be morning. He was much too tired for it to be morning, but someone was already up, moving about the room.

"Who is it?"

"Shh, Jiro. It's all right. It's just me, Kinshi. Go back to sleep."

"What are you doing up?"

"It's *all right.* Just go back to sleep."

Other questions were swimming about in Jiro's mind, but he was too tired to pull one in. Kinshi had told him to go back to sleep. He was only too grateful to obey.

When Mochida threw aside the night shutters, Jiro opened his eyes at once and turned his head to the left. To his relief Kinshi's body lay there hunched under his quilt. He first folded and put away his own quilts and then went over and shook Kinshi's shoulder.

"No," the older boy groaned. "Leave me in peace." He turned over and pulled his knees to his chin, shutting out the day.

"To the early riser come the seven advantages," Mochida sang out cheerfully.

With a sigh Kinshi pushed back the quilt. "I'll trade them all for seven hours of sleep." He sat up rubbing his face with his hands. *He looks terrible, just the way I felt yesterday,* thought Jiro.

"Master Jiro—" At the sound of Mochida's gentle voice Jiro nodded and rushed out into the courtyard to help Teiji with the fires.

As he worked he struggled with two problems: the

first, how to get word to his mother to stay off the streets;
and the second, how to discover what new mischief Kinshi
was up to. But there was a third problem—more difficult
than the other two. Somehow he must get some food and
money to his mother. If she were desperate enough to join
the night rovers, she was not likely to stay home and
meekly starve just because he told her to. Whom could he
ask for help? Only Kinshi, and Kinshi had already stolen
for him. And besides—he hardly dared put the feeling into
words even in the privacy of his own head—if he got
Kinshi into trouble, who would replace him as a foot
manipulator for Akoya? He himself might very well profit
from Kinshi's downfall. He could not in any way be the
cause of it. But what could he do? His mother was
starving, and as for his father . . . .

He got a fan from the kitchen and waved it at the
stubborn charcoal. He'd have to figure out something on
his own. Perhaps he should appeal to Yoshida directly.
The thought sent a chill through his body. Perhaps
Okada—he had said something to Jiro about all the
sickness and hunger in the land. Certainly one might
approach that kind face with the blind eyes and ask for
help for one's mother? Kinshi had once called Okada
sentimental. What could touch a sentimental old man's
heart more than a son's plea on behalf of his starving
mother? And yet—custom was a cruel dictator—Jiro still
owed Okada for two favors. The blind chanter had given
Jiro a place in the Hanaza, and in addition he had given
him the script for *The Thief of the Tokaido* when Jiro had
requested it. No, his debt to Okada was already too heavy.
He could not add to it. If there were only some way he
could ingratiate himself with Yoshida—without threaten-
ing Kinshi's position, of course—some way he could put
Yoshida in his debt at least to the extent that Jiro could
ask the master puppeteer for help. It was an unbearable

situation to be in debt to so many persons and yet have no one in debt to oneself.

The day gave no more time for thinking. Mochida had them set up the stage, and as soon as everything was ready for the performance, he sent all the boys except Kinshi back to work ripping costumes. They had been too busy the day before to finish the job, and Mochida's orderly mind was pained by the sight of incomplete tasks.

Kinshi had pleaded a need to rehearse, but as soon as they got into the dressing room, he whispered, "Forgive me, but if I don't take a nap, I won't be able to make it through today." He climbed into the cupboard on top of a pile of quilts and slid the door shut upon himself.

"I hope he's not sick." Wada's tone expressed genuine concern.

"I hope not," replied Jiro, but he kept his eyes on the seam he was ripping.

In a few minutes the sound of snoring came through the thin cupboard door. The room was silent except for the sounds from the closet.

Suddenly Mochida appeared in the doorway. "Have you seen Kinshi? Yoshida wants to rehearse something for the performance."

Jiro jumped up and ran to the door while the boys behind him raised a chorus of chatter to try to cover the telltale noise.

Half an hour before time for the performance, they dragged Kinshi out of the closet. He fought them every inch of the way, but Teiji finally got him awake by tickling the soles of his feet.

"You devil! Stop that! You know I can't stand it!"

"Shh," said Jiro. "You've got to get up. You're on stage in less than an hour."

They all helped him get into his black kimono, locate

his sandals and puppeteer's hood, and then they rushed to their own responsibilities. Jiro was standing by the left stage curtain staring out toward the audience, his mind still churning so much upon its own concerns that for several minutes he didn't fully focus on what was wrong with the scene. And then suddenly he realized it—there was hardly anyone out there. Ten people at the most— and at least five of those he could immediately identify as the police spies who showed up at any public gathering. Two of the others were so old that they had already fallen asleep where they sat.

Alarmed, he ran back to Mochida's dressing room. The left-hand manipulator was at his doorway, slipping on his stage clogs.

"There's hardly anyone out there."

Mochida sighed. "I wondered if there would be after last night."

"Last night?"

"A band of night rovers attacked Takauchi's rice market. They stole as much rice as they could carry and then burned down the building." He picked up his hood. "The merchants are probably all standing guard over their properties." He put the hood over his head, adjusting it slightly. "Come along. Yoshida will carry on as long as there's even a cockroach for an audience."

"A *paying* cockroach," Jiro mumbled under his breath, as he hurried back to his post.

As Mochida predicted, the performance went on as scheduled. "Torture by Koto" was as painstakingly and beautifully executed for ten—half of whom were watching the other half rather than the stage—as it would have been for a hundred. Despite his lack of sleep the night before, Kinshi performed well, and Jiro was glad and relieved.

After the two old men had been awakened and sent

home and the theater straightened up, Jiro took Kinshi aside. "Don't go out tonight, please."

The courtyard was already darkening, so he could not read Kinshi's expression, but the tone of his voice professed innocence. "What do you mean?"

"Oh, come now, Kinshi. You went somewhere last night after everyone was asleep."

"Oh, that." The reply was airy.

"Yes, that." He waited for Kinshi to elaborate, but he did not. Suddenly all the old affection he had had for Kinshi rushed in and blotted out the crazy mixture of feelings of the last several days. "Oh, Kinshi, it's not worth it. If Yoshida doesn't catch you, the authorities will."

"I have friends," the older boy said coldly.

"I know about those friends. They're a bunch of cutthroats. I was nearly killed . . . ." His voice trailed off. He had never told Kinshi about New Year's night.

"You worry too much, little brother. I'll be all right."

"Then let me come with you tonight."

"No. To be very honest, I don't think you'd have the belly for it." Kinshi punched Jiro's belly lightly to soften the words.

"Kinshi, I have to tell you something."

"Yes?"

"My mother. You remember?"

"Yes."

"She's one of them."

"What do you mean?"

"A night rover. She's one of the night rovers."

"How can you be sure of such a thing?"

"I heard her. I heard her voice outside the door when I was keeping guard the other night."

"You heard her voice?" Kinshi said. "You mean your mother was out there, and you didn't let her in?"

What could he say? When Kinshi reduced the

actions of that terrible night to that one question, Jiro was paralyzed with shame. He had failed his mother. It was as simple and as awful as that.

"That's why I want to go with you tonight," he said at last in a small voice. "I need to find her—to help her if it's not too late."

"No." The reply was immediate and sharp. Then more gently. "*You* cover for me here." He jabbed Jiro lightly on the shoulder. "I need your help here. *I'll* find her."

"You don't trust me, do you?"

Kinshi was quiet for a moment, then: "Perhaps another night . . . ."

He was still wide awake when Kinshi slipped out from between his quilts and tiptoed silently out of the Hanaza. Jiro turned over and over, banging his head each time against the hard pillow as though to knock away the sound of his mother's voice and the vision of her pinched and hungry face.

ELEVEN

The Proof in the Storehouse

Jiro was determined not to sleep, but his body, still tired from the vigil two nights before, betrayed him. The next thing he knew Mochida was pushing aside the night shutters, letting the bright spring morning rush into the room.

"To the early . . ." Mochida's morning proverb hung unfinished in the air. "Where is Yoshida Kinshi?" he asked instead.

Jiro forced himself to look at the empty quilts. His body felt as though it had turned into a lump of cold bean curd. He opened his dry mouth. "He-he couldn't sleep. So he went for a walk. He told me." The explanation sounded so fabricated that Jiro couldn't believe for a minute that Mochida would accept it.

But all Mochida said was, "Stupid fool. Doesn't he know how dangerous the streets are these days?" Then he turned and left the room.

Wada, Minoru, and Teiji were all staring at him, so Jiro jumped up and busily folded away both his quilts and Kinshi's. Then running out the door he called back, "Come on, Teiji. We'll be late with the fires."

His hands were trembling so that he had difficulty getting a spark from the firestones. But at last one caught the tinder, and Jiro began to blow the charcoal into flame. Physically he was preoccupied with his chores, but mentally he was going out the door of the Hanaza into Dotombori, searching the streets for Kinshi. Where was the stubborn fool? The brave and beautiful boy? North toward the river, there he saw a body facedown in the dirty water. No, no, that could not be Kinshi. He raced southward and stumbled over a body in the street. Again, not Kinshi. Kinshi was alive and well. Kinshi would laugh at his anxieties. Kinshi would—

"Yoshida wants to see you." Wada stood over him. "I'm to finish the firemaking."

Jiro jerked a nod and stood up, wiping his sooty hands on his tunic. He licked his parched lips. What in the name of heaven could he do?

Yoshida was seated cross-legged behind his low table in the dressing room. Jiro fell to his knees at the door and brought his forehead to the matting. In that position he wouldn't have to look the master in the face.

"Ah, good morning."

From his position on the floor Jiro quickly assessed the tone as somewhere on the middle of Yoshida's range of anger. So far—he breathed a little—so far things weren't too bad. "Good morning, sir," he murmured, his head still glued to the matting. "I trust you are in good health."

"My health is better than my humor at the moment."

Jiro automatically shifted the anger counter upward. He could feel the pattern of the woven matting digging into his forehead, as he fished around in his limited experience for some kind of polite reply to make to that sardonic remark, and since he came up with nothing, he kept his mouth shut.

"You may be aware that I've sent for Yoshida Kinshi to rehearse only to find that he's vanished into the mist."

"Yes," said Jiro. It seemed a safe, neutral thing to say.

"I don't suppose you have any idea of his where-abouts?"

"No, sir." Jiro dug in his forehead; he would have burrowed right through after it if he could have.

"The convenient stupidity of you boys—it's enough to try the patience of a Buddha."

"Yes, sir," replied Jiro meekly.

"And I'm not a Buddha!"

"No, sir."

"Will you get your head off the floor before it takes root?"

"Yes, sir." Jiro obediently lifted his forehead an inch. But he did not dare to raise his eyes.

"Come over here."

Jiro slid across the floor on his knees, head down, until he was about two feet from the table.

Yoshida slapped something down on it. "Do you know this?"

Jiro lifted his eyes just enough to recognize the script for *The Battle of Dannoura.* "Yes, sir."

"Be back here in an hour, ready to operate Akoya's feet. We'll practice before breakfast."

For the first time Jiro lifted his head and looked the puppeteer in the face. "Sir, I can't do that."

"You can do whatever I tell you to."

Jiro's head went back to the mat floor. His heart was pounding. "Yes, sir," he whispered. He reached up and took the script from the table. Akoya—the role for which Yoshida was famous throughout Osaka—and he, Jiro, was to do the feet. But Kinshi—What would happen to Kinshi? After all, Kinshi had gone out to look for Jiro's mother—at least that was one of Kinshi's reasons . . . .

"I need to explain, sir, about Kinshi—"

Yoshida's hand came slamming down on the table. "Kinshi must do his own explaining! You get to work before I lose my temper!"

"Yes, sir." Jiro got up and ran out of the room.

He marched straight across the courtyard and, without bothering to pretend that he was sneaking in, retrieved the key and let himself into the storehouse. He pushed over a barrel and untied the cord that secured one of the female puppets to the ceiling. This had always been Kinshi's role—he got the scripts; he got the practice puppets for everyone. Oh, Kinshi, where are you? But here was Jiro, not only walking brazenly into the storehouse and fetching the puppet, but stealing Kinshi's role onstage as well. The other boys would hate him for it. And Kinshi—Jiro dreaded going back to the dressing room. They would all know what had happened—that Yoshida had given him Kinshi's assignment. They would regard him as a traitor. Didn't he think of himself that way?

But it wasn't his fault. He had tried to explain to Yoshida. But Yoshida never accepted explanations. Everyone knew that. How could they blame him then? But they would. He knew beyond any doubt the expression that would be on each of their faces. And Kinshi's—if Kinshi ever returned. He could not bear to think of it. He was not going to practice in the dressing room—submitting himself to their hatred, feeding his own guilt—his own anxieties. But where could he hide?

He got down from the barrel. Of course. The one place no one would look for him. Upstairs in the storehouse. No one was permitted there, and as long as he came back in time to rehearse for Yoshida, Yoshida wouldn't send anyone snooping around for him.

He checked the grated door carefully. It was shut. He put the barrel back in place and then went into the dark bowels of the storehouse. The bottom stairs were in complete darkness, but he groped to the top. In order to see what he was doing he would have to go as near the tiny window as possible. It let through a thin sliver of light into the upper story.

There was a narrow path cleared to the window, but the rest of the upper floor was stacked with great trunks and chests. He wondered at first if there would be space enough for him to rehearse at all, but there was a small area near the window about three feet across and two feet deep—not what he would have wished for, but it would have to do. The rafters were low. He could hang the doll from one. With a sigh he grasped the hem of the kimono and began the manipulation of Akoya's feet in the "Torture by Koto." He didn't need the script Yoshida had given him. What irony! When you needed scripts, you were forced to steal them, but once you had the plays painfully memorized, Yoshida made a big thing of giving you the script. Jiro knew instinctively where the problems for manipulating Akoya would be—the walking, the turns, the places where she must seat herself—for the foot operator these were as crucial as the playing of the instruments would be for the other two operators. He went over and over the difficult parts, wishing he had a mirror, but beginning to trust his own feel for the movements. He was afraid to stay too long, for fear that Yoshida would be asking for him. Perhaps he could wait in the theater for the master . . . . He looked out into the courtyard. Yes, there was Teiji heading for the boys' dressing room. They would be practicing in there now, until breakfast time.

He reached up to untie the puppet. He was watching Teiji through the window, and thinking about food rather than watching what he was doing, so that his hand went up and groped about for the knot. He felt instead something quite hard. He put his fingers around it. It was smooth and shaped like a slightly flattened pipe. With a sort of mild curiosity he pulled it down off the rafter to have a look. To his surprise he found that he was grasping a sheathed samurai sword. There were, of course, no samurai in the puppet company, though some of the men, like Yoshida, were sons of samurai-retainers who had lost their positions through the death or disgrace of their masters. Actual samurai belonged to a higher social caste and were not found in theatrical troupes or business establishments. They lived off their government stipends —which meant that during these famine years most of them didn't live very well.

But what would Yoshida be doing with a samurai sword? Jiro took it to the narrow window to examine it in the light. There was a crest on the sheath—a heron with outspread wings. Where had he recently seen that crest? The skin on Jiro's scalp tingled. Images came crowding into his mind. That basket at Yoshida's house. The night Yoshida saved his life when he was said to be sick at home. The strange behavior of the puppeteer with the police officers. And here was this sword—yes, the sword stolen from the assistant magistrate, the sword Saburo had used.

He replaced it hastily on the rafter. What other evidence was hidden in the darkness of the storehouse? But no matter. The sword alone could fetch him a reward of one thousand ryo. It would be incontrovertible proof of Yoshida's guilt. He felt feverish. With that much money he could make his parents comfortable for a long time.

He pictured himself walking out the gate of the Hanaza and presenting himself to the assistant magistrate at the constabulary. "I know the true identity of Saburo." He saw the officer—he must have a new sword by now—marching with his men to the gate of the theater, stamping into Yoshida's dressing room without even removing their street clogs. Grabbing the puppeteer by the back of the neck and dragging him—*Wait*. Who would be with them to point the accusing finger? Who would climb the storehouse stairs to show them where the sword was hidden? Who would betray not only Yoshida but would be seen by all as the destroyer of the Hanaza?

And what of Kinshi? As the son of a criminal, he might be beheaded as well—and at best his life would be ruined.

Jiro sat down. There was no way that he could claim the reward money. No matter what his mother said. He was not desperate enough or greedy enough to turn Yoshida in to the authorities. He would simply have to carry this knowledge around like an uncollectable debt, like the unprofitable burden that it was.

He jumped to his feet. The sun was already high. If he was late, Yoshida would kill him. He grinned ironically. Yoshida could not be expected to appreciate the fact that he had just decided to save the master puppeteer's life.

The rehearsal went as well as could be hoped. Once Jiro's mind wandered up to the storehouse rafters and then out into the streets to look for Kinshi, but a swift kick from Yoshida's high clog brought all his senses immediately back to the stage of the Hanaza. Concentration. That was the secret of puppetry, and Jiro was enough of a puppeteer by now to be able to drive everything from his mind and body but the life of the doll in his hands.

Yoshida sent him back to get breakfast before the performance. He dreaded the thought of facing the boys (Oh, merciful Buddha—Where was Kinshi now?), but he was too hungry to skip the meal. It wouldn't do to faint onstage from lack of food, he concluded grimly.

When he went in, the three of them—Wada, Minoru, and Teiji—sat there, each with his nose in his soup bowl, shoveling in his vegetables with his chopsticks. Kinshi was not with them. No one spoke or even raised an eye when Jiro entered. So they knew about him, and as he had figured, they despised him. He got his own bowl and chopsticks, and ladled out a bowl of soup and one of rice, and dug out some pickles from the crock with his chopsticks. He sat down next to Teiji, who shifted slightly toward Minoru. Jiro tried not to notice.

The only sounds in the room were the click of the

sticks against the bowls and the slurping noises that healthy boys of their age would always make while eating. Minoru stopped eating long enough to wipe his nose on his sleeve—the hot soup always affected him—but even then, he did not look up to acknowledge that Jiro had joined them but fell doggedly to his bowl once more.

So that was the way it was going to be. Well, Jiro thought, he would have to bear it. Besides, with luck he would soon be made a foot operator officially and would be promoted to a different and larger dressing room. He could leave this cramped hole forever. He helped himself to more rice and pickles. But it was no use—he did care. And most of all he cared for Kinshi. What had happened to him? Why hadn't he come back? For one sight of that round smiling face—those ears that stuck out awkwardly, which seemed not quite evenly attached—he would give up every chance for fame and fortune that the world could offer.

Suddenly there was a thump from the closet. Minoru was seized with a coughing spell, but it came too late. Jiro jumped to the closet and pushed aside the door. There on top of the quilts was the face he had so longed to see.

"Will you shut the cursed door? You ill-formed son of a sea cucumber!" Kinshi squeezed his eyes shut and curled into a tight ball with his back to the room. Jiro closed the door, and then he began to laugh. He laughed so hard that the three other boys looked up startled, forgetting themselves. Jiro saw the corners of Teiji's mouth jerking uncontrollably. And then, one by one, they began to laugh, too, even Wada, who had determined to be angry forever, was laughing. The tears were rolling down their cheeks.

"He's all right," Jiro finally managed to gasp out. "I thought he was hurt or dead or something terrible."

The closet door opened. Kinshi's head came out. "Would you four magpies shut up and let me sleep? I've got to go on stage before long." He slammed the door back in place.

Three pairs of eyes were turned on Jiro. So they hadn't told him. He was glad. He signaled to them to keep quiet. Kinshi was going on that stage today. He wasn't sure how, but somehow he'd see to it. Jiro owed him that much.

In whispers at the far end of the room, they planned it. Kinshi would be told nothing. They would simply delay him until just before his scene was to begin. They would make sure he arrived with his hood on. By the time Yoshida realized that the foot operators had been switched, it would be too late. Of course Kinshi was taller . . . .

"H-h-he won't notice," Teiji predicted optimistically. "H-h-he's already lost in the play by the time he goes onstage."

"What about you?" Wada asked. "Yoshida will kill you afterward." It was the first time he had ever expressed to Jiro a feeling of concern for his welfare.

Jiro punched him affectionately to show Wada he was grateful. "We'll see." He shrugged his shoulders.

Their scheme worked. That is, they got Kinshi safely onstage, and although the audience was nearly as sparse as the day before, they were correct in assuming that Yoshida would never threaten a production by displaying anger or even surprise at the switch.

Yoshida waited until after supper and bath time, and then he sent for them and beat them both thoroughly with his narrow bamboo rod. But if pain can ever be said to satisfy, Jiro was satisfied by it. In one day he had overcome two temptations—one of greed and the other of ambition. He was feeling almost smug when he returned to the boys' dressing room after his turn under the rod.

Teiji brought him a cup. "W-w-we, that is, Wada s-s-s-stole some wine for you from the kitchen."

Jiro bobbed his head in a bow toward Wada. "Excuse me if I stand up to drink it."

The other three roared as though the joke had been made by Kinshi himself.

In a few minutes Kinshi joined them, gingerly patting his rear. "Ah, the ignominy," he chanted in perfect imitation of Okada, "to be so foully set upon and yet to have no means of revenge."

"What play is that from?" Minoru asked.

"A little thing"—Kinshi nodded gratefully over the cup Teiji was handing to him—"a very slight thing, known as 'The Curse of the Bamboo.' "

Minoru cocked his chubby face to one side, trying to remember such a drama. When the other boys began to laugh, he gave a puzzled little laugh, not really catching on for several seconds that there was no such play in the repertory. But when at last the point of the joke dawned, he laughed harder than anyone. Then, because it was so good to be laughing together, they all laughed some more.

"Wada is to be thanked for the wine," Jiro said when the laughter died down.

Kinshi smacked his lips appreciatively. "Excellent taste in wines, my friend."

Wada smiled. He did so love Kinshi's approval.

"Well," Kinshi said when all the wine had been drunk. "You gentlemen will forgive us if we try to find a little hot water in which to soak our pitifully abused flesh, will you not?"

He and Jiro went to the bathhouse. The fire was still alive, and they stoked it and added more wood. By the time they had washed themselves for the second time in one evening, reveling in the luxury of it, the water was warm enough to get into. Though not nearly the size of the public bath, it was large enough for both boys to get into at one time, which they did, sighing gratefully.

"Yoshida may kill us for building up the fire again at this hour," said Jiro, relaxing in the comforting warmth.

"No." Kinshi slid down until only his chin remained uncovered by the steaming water. "No, not even a dragon blows out all his smoke in a single day. Besides, I'm too tired to care whether I live or die at this point. So he wouldn't get any pleasure out of it."

"Where did you go last night?"

Kinshi raised his arm and dropped it with a *splat* upon the water.

"Kinshi."

"Oh, I heard you. Well, I'll tell you this. I saw your mother."

"You did?"

"I gave her some money and told her to go home." He paused. "I don't know if she did or not."

"No. But thank you, anyway."

"I told her it was from you."

"But—"

"Well, I couldn't say where it was really from, now could I?"

"No." Where was it really from? he wanted to ask but could not. "Kinshi."

"Yes?"

"Don't go out anymore."

"I have to," Kinshi said quietly. "There is no one else."

"No one else?"

"Who cares. Who can help." The look in the older boy's eyes was the one which appeared during his confrontations with Yoshida. "Who can help the night rovers," he said. "No one else even thinks of them as human."

"What if—" Jiro spoke slowly, thinking out his plan as he spoke. "Suppose, I could arrange for you to meet Saburo . . . ."

Kinshi snorted. "Saburo? You puffball. Where?"

"Just listen a minute. Suppose I could find him, and

. . . and"—he hurried on, anticipating Kinshi's laugh— "suppose I could arrange for you to talk to him about your plan to help the night rovers."

"Jiro, be sensible. Even if you could find him and I could talk to him, do you think for a moment that a man like that would listen to *me*?"

"He might." *Not*, thought Jiro uncomfortably, *that he ever has before*. "He might. Wouldn't it be worth trying?"

Kinshi made a funny clucking noise in his throat. "You're crazy."

"All right. Maybe so, but promise me you'll give me time—a week. If I don't get you in touch with Saburo in a week's time, then I won't try to talk you out of whatever it is you're up to, but at least give me a week."

"Jiro." Kinshi shook his head incredulously.

"Give me a week."

"Two days. I have friends. People who are counting on me. They won't wait a week."

"All right," Jiro agreed reluctantly. "Two days, but you have to swear—"

"No, I'm not going to swear anything. I promise to try. But I've already made promises that may be more urgent than this one. It's crazy," he said again. "You know the only reason I'm taking you seriously at all is because of what you did today. I owe you something for that."

"No. It was *my* mother you helped."

"Well, we won't go on counting debts and counter-debts like a pair of polite women." Kinshi climbed out and grasping his small towel at either end began rubbing his body briskly. "I won't go out tonight anyway. So don't keep awake all night playing watchdog."

Jiro dried himself and slipped into one of the bath kimono. Tomorrow he would have to figure out how to accomplish his crazy plan, but for tonight he was too tired to do any more thinking.

TWELVE

A Matter of Life and Death

Jiro woke up before anyone else with a sense of urgency about the day that he couldn't immediately identify. He lay for a minute in the darkness, sending his mind back to the previous day until he remembered what it was that he had to do.

When he thought of what lay ahead, he shivered and snuggled farther under his quilt. He wasn't anxious for this day to begin. *Selfish, selfish child.* That's what his mother would say. But it was not that he was selfish or so wrapped up in his own concerns that he could not proceed. It was, rather, that in the enormity of the problems that faced him he had no inkling as to how to proceed.

He set himself to organizing his situation. First of all there was Kinshi, his friend. If someone didn't stop him, Kinshi would get himself arrested or killed, perhaps both. Then there was his mother. The gods alone knew what she was up to—but it didn't take much imagination to realize that she was desperate either for herself or for Hanji and was likely to bring disaster upon the three of them. Next his father— When Jiro thought of his father, a feeling of helplessness washed over him. If only he knew where Hanji was and what was happening to him. But surely someone would have come—Taro or Taro's father, Sano

—to tell him if his father was dead or even if he was much sicker than before. He put aside the painful questions about his father and turned to consideration of Yoshida. Yoshida was the key to all his difficulties. But he was not a key that Jiro might slip into a lock and easily turn.

How to approach Yoshida? That was the problem. He must figure out a way to get to Yoshida and lay open to him the facts Jiro knew or had guessed. But he must do it in such a way that Yoshida would listen to him. Yoshida's responses were immediate and usually angry. If Jiro's first sentence—even his first word—struck the master puppeteer in the wrong way, he was likely to throw the boy out on his nose.

Jiro had a weapon of sorts. He knew about the sword in the rafters of the storehouse. But he didn't know how to make use of his knowledge. Did one march in arrogantly and say, "Yoshida, I know you are Saburo the bandit, and if you don't do what I say, I'll turn you in to the authorities." Jiro almost laughed out loud at the idea. Yoshida was as likely to kill him as to spit, and how would his death benefit either Kinshi or Isako? Besides, Jiro had never been completely convinced by the samurai tradition which held it to be a noble thing to throw one's life away for the sake of those to whom one is bound by the ties of duty or affection. He was very attached to his scraggly body and the somewhat less than grand spirit that animated it.

For a moment he pictured himself stretched out, washed and dressed for burial. His mother knelt beside him weeping, sobbing her heart out. Kinshi was there, too, grim-faced with anguish. They knew he had sacrificed all for them. It was rather beautiful, but not quite beautiful enough to win him over. No, he had no desire to die even a magnanimous or romantic death.

But that was not the important thing anyhow. The important thing was that Yoshida must be made to listen and somehow be persuaded to help. It wouldn't do simply to tell Yoshida that Kinshi was involved with the night rovers. Yoshida would just beat his son and forbid him to go out—which might be all that it would take to drive Kinshi permanently into the streets.

Jiro had told Kinshi that he would arrange for him to meet Saburo, so that Kinshi could talk to him about his plan to help the night rovers. The meeting not only had to be arranged; it had to be set up so skillfully that Yoshida would at least give Kinshi a respectful hearing. But it was harder to picture Yoshida giving Kinshi a respectful hearing than it had been to picture his own funeral. Watonai tamed the tiger in *The Battles of Coxinga*, but Watonai was a fierce warrior armed with his mother's magic amulet. Jiro was a skinny boy, whose supernatural gift from his mother consisted of a curse upon the day she bore him. The only argument that might persuade Yoshida was at the same time the most dangerous one—the fact that the assistant magistrate's sword had been discovered in the storehouse.

At about the same moment that Mochida opened the room to the still reluctant morning, the idea that Jiro had been struggling for dawned in his mind. He needed an intermediary—someone he and Yoshida both trusted—to approach the puppeteer. Someone, as well, who cared about Kinshi.

Mochida was calling them to attend the new day, but before he could snatch off the quilts, Jiro jumped up and folded his and put them away. What about Mochida? The left-hand operator met every test. He was respected by all, and he certainly cared for Kinshi. But he was not Yoshida's peer. The difference in position would make Mochida hesitant and Yoshida arrogant. That was a real concern. There was no one on the west side of the Hanaza who was Yoshida's equal and who could speak to him frankly without fear of the puppeteer's well-known wrath.

And on the east side, who was there who cared whether Kinshi or Jiro's mother lived or died? The chanters and musicians lived in their own world and only deigned to step down into that of the puppeteers when the practice of their art demanded it. They thought of the puppeteers in much the same way a healthy man regards his digestive system—as necessary but hardly worth discussing. The only thing the east side required of the west side was that it function properly and provide an adequate background for the execution of what *they* considered the true arts—chanting and music.

But there was one notable exception on the east side. There was one person who, if he were willing, could speak to Yoshida for Jiro. One person who also cared if Yoshida Kinshi lived or died. That person was the blind Okada. He had once been Yoshida's master. Surely Yoshida still owed him something for that. Yes, Yoshida would listen to Okada.

Why hadn't Jiro thought of him before? It was perfect. He would confide the whole situation to Okada. The old man would know instinctively how to appeal to both of the Yoshidas, father and son.

Jiro did his chores in the courtyard with one eye out for Tozo, Okada's favorite in the east wing. When the boy came out to pick up his master's breakfast, Jiro stopped him.

"Good morning," he said in his politest tone. "Please forgive me for bothering you at such a busy time."

Tozo's eyebrows went up questioningly, but he nodded his head, keeping his lovely features expressionless. He was really too beautiful for a boy. "Yes?"

"Forgive me for imposing again, but I need to see Okada today." Jiro licked his lips. "It's very important."

"I don't think it's possible today," Tozo said, not unkindly. "The master is very tired, and he has a difficult performance ahead."

"Yes, I know. I wouldn't ask—except it's a matter of life and death."

Tozo smiled—a tiny smile that he immediately forced into a grimace—but Jiro caught it and knew that he had overstated his case, and now he was not being taken seriously by the gentle young musician.

"Tozo, believe me. I must see Okada." What could he say? "Tell him that if he has any affection for Yoshida Kinshi to see me, please."

"Yoshida Kinshi?"

"It involves both Yoshidas. Tell him if he cares what happens to either of them . . . ." He could feel the strain in his own voice, so he stopped talking. Tozo would write him off as an emotional boy if he were not careful. If he could only send a note to Okada! Blindness was such a wretched handicap.

Tozo began to move away. "You'll tell him?" Jiro called out.

"Oh, yes. But I can't promise . . . ."

Jiro jerked his head in a nervous little bow. *Please, Tozo,* he begged silently, *make him see me.*

He finished his chores, the practice session, and his own breakfast, and still there was no word from Okada. Jiro tried to figure out some other course to take, but his mind refused to cooperate. It was as though he had entrusted all his treasure to one ship, and if it did not reach port, ruin was inevitable.

But when at last Tozo came out to fetch his master's midmorning tea, he went over to where Jiro stood, pouring boiling water over the tea leaves in the individual pots that the apprentices would then take to the various rooms.

"Okada says he will see you, if you will come right away."

Jiro straightened. "Minoru," he yelled. The fat boy

who was halfway across the courtyard with a pot of tea turned.

"Finish this for me, will you? I'll be right back." Jiro raced across the courtyard, and then, remembering himself, stopped at the entrance to the east side, dropped his clogs, and waited barefoot for Tozo to catch up. He followed the young samisen player down the hall to Okada's dressing room and stood outside, shifting from one foot to the other, while the boy took in the master chanter's tea and told the old man of his presence.

Finally Tozo came out. "He'll see you now."

"Thank you, Tozo."

"It's nothing."

Jiro went just inside the door and knelt. The blind man's face turned immediately although Jiro had not been conscious of making a sound.

"Ah, Hanji's son, is it? Come in, little puppeteer."

"I'm afraid"—Jiro forced himself to go through the polite ritual—"I'm afraid I'm interrupting you at a very busy time."

"For life and death I bend my inflexible schedule a little." The reciter was poking fun at him, but it didn't matter; Jiro was in the door now. He would just have to convince Okada of the seriousness of things. He moved across the room so that he could speak quietly, though Okada could probably have understood a whisper from the doorway.

It was hard to know where to begin, but he chose to begin with Kinshi because that was where his own heart lay.

"And he is going out every night, or almost every night."

The old man was drinking his tea, but he was listening intently. "He told you he was trying to organize the night rovers?"

"Not in so many words." Jiro leaned forward. "He

seems to think that only someone like Saburo would have the ability to do that. I don't really know what he thinks he can do by himself. I'm just afraid he'll get himself killed."

Okada nodded. "That's not unlikely. But if you can't dissuade him from these outings, do you think he'll listen to an old blind man?"

This was the hard part. Jiro licked his lips. "Kinshi wants to meet Saburo," he began.

"So does half the country." Okada smiled, little crinkles appearing around his sightless eyes. "Poor little Kinshi."

"I made a bargain with him," Jiro continued. "If I will arrange for him to talk with Saburo about helping the night rovers, he won't go out on the streets. But he only gave me two days. He won't wait longer than that."

"So you are to produce the elusive Saburo for Kinshi in just two days?" Okada's smile broadened. "Yoshida was right about you. You do not lack spirit." *When had the two masters discussed him*, Jiro wondered, *and why?* "You may totally lack common sense, making such an agreement, but not spirit." It was another gentle poke, but Jiro ignored it.

"Okada, this will come as a shock, but the reason I've come to you is that you could arrange this introduction." Jiro paused to let the words gather strength. "You are very close to the man known as Saburo."

The blind man put down his teacup, carefully using his left hand to guide it into the lacquer saucer.

"You must explain your meaning to me."

Step by step, Jiro told Okada the observations and experiences from the time he had seen the basket hat in Yoshida's house to, finally, his finding the sword in the rafters of the storehouse. Okada sat quietly throughout Jiro's recitation, his expression unchanging. When Jiro, breathless from the telling, finished at last, he said quietly,

"You realize, my son, that you are lodging a very serious charge against Yoshida."

"Yes, sir."

"His life is in your hands."

"I realize that, sir."

"And you are not tempted to betray him? The reward is considerable." The blind man fingered the embossed pattern on his teacup. "You do not pretend any great love for the man."

"But Kinshi . . ."

"Ah, that's it. It's your love for his son that stops you."

"I would never do anything that might threaten Kinshi. But I'm afraid he's going to bring harm to himself. That's why I came to you."

Okada nodded. "You were right to come."

"Then you'll talk to Yoshida?"

Okada sighed. "You are not asking me to do an easy thing."

"No, I know, sir."

Okada smiled slightly. "You know the temper of the man, I think."

"Yes, sir."

"He cannot be approached too carefully."

"No, sir."

"And if he is indeed Saburo, he is more dangerous than you imagine. Remember Saburo's warning in the theater that night? If he thought someone might betray him, he might feel he had no choice but to silence that person."

Somewhere inside Jiro, he felt an icy trickle of fear.

"It might be too great a risk—or he might see it as too great a risk—entrusting not only his own life, but the lives of his entire band to one person of whom he could not be quite sure."

"Yoshida might feel that way about me." Jiro swallowed hard to keep the fear from seeping into his voice. "But not about *you*, sir. You could talk to him. You could ask him to help the night rovers. He would trust you."

"Yes—he ought to trust me. I was his master in the old days at Takemoto, did you know?"

"Yes, Kinshi told me."

Suddenly the old man leaned forward, his sightless face bright. "Would you help me?"

"I, sir?"

"Yes. If I had that basket—or better yet—the sword lying here on my table when he walked in . . . ."

"Of course." How clever the old man was. "You would have an advantage over him before a word was said."

"Do you think it would work?" Okada sounded like a child eager for approval.

"Oh, yes." Jiro jumped to his feet. "I'll get it for you."

Okada cocked his head thoughtfully. "Perhaps I should send Tozo. We don't know how the man might react if he caught you in the storehouse."

"I've been in before. No one seems to notice me any more than they notice Kinshi going in. And I know just where to put my hand on the sword."

"You're sure?"

"Yes. I have no responsibilities during the last acts. I'll go then. Nobody will be paying any attention to me. Don't worry. I'll be all right. Then I'll just slip in here with it." Jiro looked around the room. "Where shall I hide it?"

"There's a stack of cushions to my right, isn't there?"

"But they're not wide enough; the sword would stick out the side."

"Bother," the old man muttered.

"What about under the bedding in the closet?"

"Tozo's always poking around in there and in my chest. Besides, I couldn't find it so easily myself. Blindness

is not so much an affliction as a wretched inconvenience."
He sat quietly as though mentally reviewing the room for
hiding places. "Behind the night shutters?"

"Would Tozo try to close them before you get it
out?"

Okada clicked his tongue impatiently. "Oh, it won't
be for long. Just pull out one of the cushions to cover the
tip. I'll try to keep Tozo busy and out of here until tonight
after the performance is over."

"You'll talk to Yoshida tonight?"

"The sooner the better, wouldn't you say?"

Jiro bumped his head to the matting. "I don't know
how to thank you, sir."

Okada waved away the words. "It is for all our sakes,"
he said kindly.

Jiro hardly noticed that the other boys were disgrun-
tled at him for leaving his midmorning chores for them to
do, such a great weight had been lifted from his shoulders.
Okada would take care of everything, he felt confident of
it.

"You missed your tea," Kinshi said. "I tried to save
some, but the other boys said that since they had done all
your work, they should drink up your share."

"That seems fair," Jiro replied cheerfully.

Kinshi frowned. "Your black gloom cloud seems to
have sprouted rainbows."

Jiro grinned. "Does it?" But the conversation was not
pursued because it was time for Kinshi to go and put on
his kimono and get ready for the performance.

In the east wing's chief dressing room, the blind
chanter had called for Tozo. It was a different voice from
the one Jiro knew best. But a chanter has a thousand
voices.

"Tozo, take word to Yoshida that I am ill. Toyotake
can go on for me."

"Yes, sir."

"And Tozo . . . ."

"Yes?"

"Send for Hanji. A problem has arisen with his son."

THIRTEEN

The Master Puppeteer

Jiro retrieved the key and carefully unlocked the grating. From the theater he could hear Toyotake, one of the senior reciters, chanting the act. No one would be watching the storehouse at such a busy time of the afternoon, but he instinctively turned around and searched the courtyard before he slid in and closed the grating behind him. He stuck the key in his sash and made his way through the musty darkness toward the staircase at the rear of the building. He wasn't conscious of being nervous, but he realized that he was sweating and that a pulse in his temple was thumping painfully. He crept up the dark steps, putting his hands on the stair above and climbing like a cat, squinting his eyes in an attempt to accustom them quickly to the darkness.

He made his way through the narrow open space toward the front of the storehouse and the light from the single window. Once there he stood on tiptoe and ran his fingers across the top of the broad rafter to locate the sword, but it was harder to locate than he'd thought. Finally he lifted a small chest from one of the stacks of chests, and put it down in front of the window and slightly to the side of the center rafter, and climbed up to look.

The sword was gone.

He tried to swallow his panic. It must be there. It was just too dark to see the black-enameled sheath. He ran his outspread hands all up and down the central rafter and came up with nothing except very dusty palms. It had to be the central rafter. The rest of the room was piled almost to the beams with boxes and chests. There was no way he could be mistaken about where the sword had been. Someone had moved it.

He climbed down and sat upon the chest. His hands were halfway to his face before Jiro remembered how dirty they were. He wiped them methodically on the sides of his trousers. What was he going to do? Without the sword, Okada might not even believe him, and even if he did, they had no evidence with which to confront Yoshida. There was the basket, but he had seen that months ago with a fall arrangement in it. Since then Mrs. Yoshida would have changed the alcove theme at least twice, for the different seasons, and there was no way quickly to find where the basket might be stashed away. Time—he had no time—he would be missed backstage before long. How could he even slip away for a few minutes to look?

He had to go. He got up, put the chest back, and made his way through the narrow passageway toward the steps. Jiro put his left hand out to steady himself in the darkness and looked down. When he did so, his blood froze. For there at the bottom of the staircase, just barely distinguishable in the darkness, someone was coming. By the shape he knew that the person was wearing a puppeteer's hood.

There was no place to hide, but Jiro instinctively backed into the narrow passageway.

The hooded figure moved on up the steps. When it reached the top and turned toward him, Jiro could see that it carried a male puppet. The left arm and legs dangled lifelessly from the doll, but the person had placed his hands at the neck and right arm and was manipulating the puppet in such a way that the doll seemed to be peering first to the left and then to the right in search of something or someone.

Jiro had backed his way almost to the window when the puppet stopped and seemed to fix its gaze on him.

"Ah," it said. "There you are. I've been looking everywhere for you." There was something in the voice that seemed familiar to Jiro, but especially with the added cloak of darkness around the puppeteer, Jiro could not escape the impression that the voice was coming from the wooden face.

"Do you know," it continued, "what a dangerous thing curiosity can be?"

Jiro flattened himself against the window, but the puppet stayed where it was. "Remember the story of the peasant girl who was courted by a handsome suitor? She was not content that a highborn personage would deign to notice an ordinary girl like herself. She wanted to know what his name was and who his noble parents might be and where his ancestral home might stand." The puppet moved slightly and the light from the window caught something shining in its right hand. Jiro recognized it at once as a puppet sword, which like all the props of the Hanaza were perfect in every detail—just slightly smaller than the originals.

"The girl, as you will remember, asked her nurse how she might learn her lover's identity. And the old woman gave her a needle—as sharp as my sword here. The needle was threaded, and as her lover left, she stuck it deep into his garments. Then giving him a head start, she and the nurse followed the thread. It led them out of the city and deep, deep, into the forest, disappearing at last into a cave."

Jiro knew the story, of course, but he waited, his throat dry, for the puppet to finish it.

"The old nurse lit a lamp, and the two curious

women went into that cave—and what should they find but an enormous serpent writhing in pain, the needle pierced deep into its throat."

The puppet began to writhe, and holding the sword before it, came toward Jiro in a kind of horrifying dance. "Poor little Jiro." It was those words that made Jiro recognize the voice. "Why are you frightened? It is you who hold the needle to the serpent's flesh."

"Okada?" Jiro could hardly whisper the name. "Okada?"

"You wanted to get word to Saburo, did you not?"

"Yes, but . . ."

The hooded figure bowed.

"But how?"

"How can an old blind man be the dashing Saburo?" The chanter put down the puppet and lifted the hood from his head. "Ah, little Jiro. You make the mistake they all do. Yoshida is famous throughout Osaka as the master puppeteer of the Hanaza, when it is I who manipulate Yoshida." He laughed his funny kind of sputtering laugh. "Yes, Saburo has many puppets. The whole east wing belongs to him as well as Yoshida and a chosen few on the outside who have sworn their life's blood to his cause. But Saburo is only one. I alone am the master puppeteer."

Jiro stood, his back against the thin window, hardly breathing, as if by not making a sound he could remain invisible to the blind man, but Okada took another step forward toward him, the puppet's sword glinting in his hand.

"What am I to do? I come into my storehouse to find a mouse nibbling away at my treasure? What does the master do when he catches a mouse with its jaws sunk deep into—"

Jiro did not wait. He snatched the chest nearest him and threw it down between himself and the chanter. He grabbed another and piled it on top. Then scrambling

upon them to the rafters, he swung himself up like a monkey and slid across above Okada's head. When he was past him, he jumped from the rafter and pushed more boxes and chests into the passageway. The blind man had dropped the sword to the floor and was flailing his arms around helplessly, trying to find a way out of the trap that Jiro was throwing up around him.

"Jiro, I command you. Wait. Wait—wait, I say."

But Jiro was down the stairs and out the grating. He slammed it shut, and then, half in panic, swung closed from either side the giant iron doors and threw the heavy bolt in place. He, Jiro, had Saburo the bandit locked behind iron doors, and all he could think of was that poor old man thrashing his arms about, crying piteously for him to wait.

He would have to find Kinshi. Kinshi would know what to do. He ran across the courtyard, but just as he got to the door, someone snatched his arm.

"Where in the devil have you been?" Mochida's usually placid features were contorted with anger.

"I-I—"

"Yoshida Kinshi's disappeared and you have to replace him on Akoya's feet. Okada's ill and can't go on. Believe me"—Mochida smiled grimly—"the master is in a proper mood, so take care." All the time he was speaking Mochida was dressing Jiro in the black kimono. When he finished, he stuffed a hood over Jiro's head and shoved him toward the stage entrance where Yoshida and the left-hand manipulator were waiting.

Jiro grasped Akoya's hem between his fingers and bent into position. *Ow.* Some god saved him from crying aloud as Yoshida's high clog banged into his ankle. The next second the three of them were gliding onto the stage behind the puppet. The performance of "Torture by Koto" had begun.

FOURTEEN

The Smashings

If he lived to be one hundred and became a master puppeteer with a theater of his own, he would never again rival the performance he gave that day. Had his concentration wavered for one instant from the performance, he would have gone to pieces, so he drove himself into the depths of it. He was like a pearl diver, leaving the world of light and air far behind, plunging toward the treasure at the bottom of the sea.

When the scene was over at last, he snatched off his hood and kimono and dropped them to the backstage floor, then raced toward the alley door. He could hear someone calling his name as he lifted the bolt, but he pretended not to hear. Outside it was already dusk, but still the summer heat clung in the air.

"Jiro!" Tozo had caught the back of his tunic and was holding on. "Where are you going?"

"Let go. I have to go." But the slender youth was stronger than he appeared.

"Where's my master?" Tozo demanded; his expression had shed any hint of feminine softness. "You saw him last, didn't you?"

"Merciful god," Jiro murmured. The old man might be dead in that airless place. "Let me go, and I'll tell you."

Tozo loosened his grasp.

"He's—he's locked in the storehouse."

"What do you mean?"

But Jiro left him to puzzle it out alone. His responsibility was to find Kinshi. And he had to do so before Okada had a chance to send someone out looking for Jiro himself.

As soon as he was out of sight of the Hanaza, he slowed his pace. Where was Kinshi? With the night rovers, he guessed. And the night rovers would go where they thought they could get food. The only area of the city with plenty of food was the merchant district. He could think of no better plan than to head that way, keeping his eyes and ears open for signs of his friend.

Suddenly he heard the clanging of the fire gong. Trouble had not even waited for darkness. Up ahead in the next block he could see the members of the neighborhood fire brigade pouring into the street. He ran to catch up with them, and as he did so, he could hear the gongs sounding from the rooftops of every fire brigade in the district.

The air was soon full of smoke, and up ahead fingers of fire pierced the evening sky. Above the shouts of the firemen and even above the clamor of the gongs, there was a cacophony of banging and crashing and strange unearthly cries as though hell had unleashed all its goblins.

When he turned the next corner, he saw them. The night rovers were armed with sticks or clubs—some with bamboo clothespoles, others with brooms. Some carried lamps; others, torches. Like a pack of rabid animals they raced about, smashing everything before them. And if any merchant or fireman dared oppose one of them, three or four of the pack would turn snarling upon the enemy until they had beaten him senseless to the ground.

He watched as a group chopped through wooden night shutters with axes and meat cleavers, and then an old woman flung an oil lamp through the opening. Screams came from within as the fire caught the paper doors, and within a few seconds flames were leaping up from the roof.

The night rovers roared with laughter and battered down what remained of the shutters. They ran into the flames and came running out again, laden down, still laughing and shouting to one another, showing off their loot for a moment; then they dropped it into the street to smash and burn again.

Jiro stood in the street and yelled as loud as he could: "Kinshi! Kinshi-i-i!" He might as well have screamed at a typhoon.

A fireman bumped his arm and told him angrily to get off the street, but he stayed, and when the rioters moved on, he followed them, trying to jostle his way in close enough, past firemen and dazed onlookers, to see the faces of the mad men and women.

Gradually it dawned on him that it was not only this street or this band of night rovers—the whole city was blazing. Osaka had been a city straddling a volcano for too many years. Now, at last, the oppressed had erupted and were determined to destroy the city that had tyrannized them. Jiro left and walked to the next street where the scene of violence and mindless destruction was being repeated. All night he went from street to street, calling Kinshi's name and trying to catch a glimpse of his face in the light of the fires that seemed to be sweeping the city.

When he saw someone lying in the dark shadows of the street, he knelt down to examine the face, or if they lay, as they often did, facedown, with a bloody wound matting the hair, he would call the name gently—if the person appeared to be breathing—and turn the body over if it were lifeless.

By morning the smell of singed flesh was everywhere. He was stumbling with exhaustion and discouragement.

But he was aware that the noises of the night were dying down. For the moment the fire brigades were evident in force and seemed to be fighting the fires unhindered. The police were moving in as well, capturing those night rovers who had been injured or were too old or too young or too fatigued to outrun them.

A man in a fireman's coat with a fireman's straw hat covering his features tilted his head questioningly toward Jiro, and with a start, Jiro realized that the man might be meaning to question him. When the fireman started to cross the street to him, Jiro turned and ran. Despite his earlier exhaustion, he was flooded with new strength and able quickly to outdistance the older man now running in pursuit. Jiro soon left the flaming business district behind him. Instinct took him to the narrow streets of the artisans and brought him, his eyes blurred, his chest bursting with pain, to his father's shop. He leaned heavily against the door, without a voice to call out.

Suddenly Jiro looked up to see that the fireman had followed him, but the boy was too tired to move. He slid to the cobblestones and sat there waiting for the man to arrest him. The man came and leaned over him. "I hoped I'd find you here," he said.

Jiro looked up into his father's face. It was too much. The boy put his head down on his drawn-up knees and began to cry like a baby. Hanji shoved the unlocked door open and helped Jiro to his feet.

"You were out looking for your mother, weren't you?"

Though it was not really true, Jiro was too spent to explain; he nodded and stumbled into the house after his father. The older man took a vial from his tunic and poured both of them out a little cup of rice wine. When the clear liquor had burned his throat, Jiro found his voice.

"I was looking not only for Mother but for Yoshida Kinshi. Did you see him?"

Hanji shook his head negatively. "Okada said nothing about him—only you."

"Okada?"

"Yes, he sent word that you were out and that I should find you." Hanji drank down the last of his wine. "We were both worried, of course, that you should be in the streets like that. I didn't know until I stopped by here that your mother was out as well."

"Do you know why Okada is worried about me?"

"He is a kind man," Hanji said without looking Jiro in the face. His father was one of Saburo's band. Suddenly Jiro was sure of it.

"You haven't been sick, have you?"

Hanji didn't answer immediately. He got up and washed out the wine cups. "I am sorry," he said, his words careful and deliberate, "for the pain I have caused you and your mother." With his long artist's fingers he pulled a cloth from a peg and wiped the cups.

"You've been working for him all this time?"

Hanji did not look up. "There are many of us."

"What did he"—Jiro's voice cracked in midsentence —"did he tell you about me?"

"He told me that you were a brave and spirited boy—that I should be proud of you. I believed him," his father added quietly.

It was not an answer that Jiro could puzzle out. It might mean that Okada had not told his father about the storehouse or it might mean that his father knew but was not telling him. If Hanji had sworn allegiance to Saburo— it was like *The Thief of the Tokaido*, was it not? Joman's son is cheered because he dies for his father. Hanji would be cheered for sacrificing his son for his master's sake.

Jiro got up. "I have to go," he said. "I still have to find Kinshi—and Mother."

"I'll go with you."

"No, no," Jiro said quickly. "Please, no. Tell Okada that I will come back to the theater as soon as I have found them. I promise, I swear I will come back, and whatever Okada wishes, I will submit to it. Just let me find them first."

His father seemed to hesitate. Then he took off the fireman's coat he was wearing. "Here, take this and the hat," he said. "They'll give you some measure of protection against the authorities."

Jiro put them on obediently, then bowed, a little stiffly, to his father.

"Bear yourself carefully," his father said at the front entrance.

"And you." Jiro nearly choked on the reply.

Hanji watched his son disappear around the corner before, with practiced stealth, he left the house.

FIFTEEN

Fireman of Namba Cho Brigade

The fireman's coat was too large for him. His fingertips were several inches short of the ends of the sleeves, and he was torn between trying to push up the sleeves so that his hands would show, which meant he had to hold his arms close to his body in an unnatural fashion, or letting the sleeves fall loose and long and hoping no one would notice. The largeness of the hat was not a problem. It really covered his face. Neither the police officers who had been at the Hanaza or Okada's men would be able to spot him easily.

He walked along, his heart beating so noisily and painfully that at first he heard the cries and clangor of the streets distantly like the background pot beating behind stage at the Hanaza. But the streets of Osaka were still teeming with evil intent, and if Jiro had had less within to fear, he would have been acutely aware of all that was swirling about him. Every ronin and ragpicker—even the once respectable craftsmen—the always hungry and the newly starved—were crawling over the body of the city, bent on destroying it.

Jiro was jostled and shoved at every step. The crowds were not traveling in a single direction but were pushing from every way, rushing narrow-eyed to anywhere or nowhere, maggots swarming on a two-week corpse.

And for these Kinshi had compassion! The thought of Kinshi—strong and pure—laughing at himself and poking loving fun at others—Kinshi, the only truly good person left in the world—now that Jiro knew that his own father had deserted his mother to become a bandit—Kinshi, being crushed, perhaps killed for such as these—that ronin there—his face and beard encrusted with filth, carrying under each arm bolts of silk—a looter, a thief, and with that sword at his belt, perhaps a murderer as well. How could Kinshi want to help such a one as that?

As though reading Jiro's mind, the ronin turned. He fixed his eyes on Jiro, and using the bolts of material as wooden elbows, he jabbed and forced his way across the street to face the boy. With a sweep of a bolt he sent Jiro's hat sailing across the heads of the crowd.

"Fireman!" He used the word like an obscenity, and then raising his leg kicked it under Jiro and sent him sprawling against the crowd, which moved back quickly, allowing him to fall on the cobblestones. A big foot came down immediately on Jiro's chest. The ronin leaned over and smiled a nasty smile. "I've got me another fireman," he said, and then he raised his head and his voice. "Hey! Hey, everyone. I've got me another fireman."

"What's your score, Master ronin?"

"Four. Four since last night, and everybody knows four is a very unlucky number, right?"

"Right!"

"Never stop with four, Master ronin!"

"Five is an ideal number!"

"Shall I hold your silk?"

The ronin jerked away from this offer. "I don't need help." He shifted the bolt from under his right arm to his left and grasped both bolts tenaciously. Then standing with one foot on either side of Jiro's hips, he drew his long sword. "Quick like a chicken?" He drew the blade lightly across Jiro's neck. "Or more elegantly?"—the sword crisscrossed Jiro's chest and belly—"Like a pig or an ox?"

"Like a pig!" a man's voice shouted.

"A pig!" another echoed.

The ronin grinned. "A pig it shall be."

Lying there stunned, perhaps initially by the fall, Jiro felt as he had at New Year's that the scene was not, could not be real. But the touch of the cold steel across his neck jarred him to alertness. He was not ready to die. He had to find Kinshi and his mother. If Okada wished to have him killed then—but that was beyond his powers. This was not. While the ronin played the scene out for the crowd, Jiro took the moment to reach up with both hands, grab the ronin's right leg, and jerk with all his might. And as the big man tottered off-balance, Jiro yelled, "Get the silk. It's worth a fortune!"

Both bolts were gone by the time the ronin's body hit the pavement, and so was Jiro, leaving the crowd shrieking derisively at the braggart who had now neither silk nor fireman to boast of.

Fear gave Jiro the strength to push his way through the mobs to an alley where he found room to strip himself of the fireman's coat. Was that the way his father had wanted him to die? But Jiro dismissed the thought. After all, his father had worn the coat himself. It would seem to depend on the circumstances whether the coat would be a protection or a threat. He folded it carefully and stuck it under the flap of his tunic.

If only he could keep to the alleys, he would be safe. But unfortunately the alleys as often as not dead-ended into the side of a building or a garden wall, and Jiro would have to make his way back into the main streets where the looters, arsonists, and smashers whirled about in chaotic and perilous crosscurrents.

But he was not here to keep himself safe. He was here to find Kinshi and Isako, and somehow he must figure out how to accomplish this. The daylight was in his favor. He could see as he hadn't been able to the night before. But in this second wave of violence the crowds had grown in size and in belligerence, so that the search itself was far more hazardous. Last night there had been at least an effort on the part of the authorities to control the mobs. Since leaving Hanji's shop, he had not seen any police or police assistants at all. They did well to keep off the streets. If people were attacking firemen, what would they do to police? But early this morning they had been arresting people. Jiro was pricked by a tiny needle of hope. If Kinshi and Isako had been arrested, they might be safe.

Now that he had a goal it seemed easier to make his way through the streets. He would go directly to the constabulary and ask for assistance there. After all, dressed in his fireman's coat, he was one of them, wasn't he? Jiro waited until he was almost at the constabulary gate before putting on the coat again.

He was greeted respectfully by an underassistant magistrate, a stout, pleasant man, who told him what a courageous role his fire brigade had played the night before and questioned him closely about a number of close calls. Fortunately Jiro's ignorance about the Namba Cho Fire Brigade was taken for modesty, and he was praised lavishly and led into the courtyard—after proper approval had been gained from the officer in charge—to see if he could find his relatives.

Even with the open air above, the courtyard stank worse than a stable. It was jammed with people. Here and there an injured person was stretched out on the stones, but for most there was hardly room to sit down, and when someone moved, the movement rippled through the yard, so that people were falling and stumbling across the prone figures. Jiro stood with the officer at the edge of the crowd and tried to scan each face.

"Do you see them?" the underassistant asked.

"It's impossible. There are too many people here. I can't tell."

The officer disappeared into the building and came back with a stool. He patted the top. "Climb up here," he said. "Maybe they'll see you."

Jiro stepped up on the stool. Dozens of sullen eyes turned toward him. It took him a minute to realize that it was the Namba Cho uniform. They hated his uniform. He tried to look stern and stare them all down.

"Jiro! I'm here!" The scream came from somewhere in the crowd. "It's my boy! He's come to get me!"

There was an angry murmuring in response. The police officer roughly pushed back a path with his iron rod, and Jiro followed him to the place from which his mother's cry had come. Just behind Isako stood—yes, Jiro was sure, it must be Kinshi, though the posture seemed peculiarly humble for Kinshi. His head was bowed, and a large woven hat, such as the samurai wore for disguise in the pleasure district, covered his features.

Jiro willed his face to show no expression. "They are both here," he said to the officer. "This is my brother, as well. I can't thank you enough for your kind help."

"You mustn't say that," said the policeman. "Not after the bravery of your brigade last night. We are only too glad . . . ." He bowed slightly to Isako and Kinshi. "You may both go," he said quietly. "But please do not stir up the crowd."

Isako reached behind her and grasped Kinshi's left sleeve. "Come with me," she said.

The underassistant magistrate again forced a path through the human forest, and Jiro shoved his mother and Kinshi ahead of him without a word. They were almost safe, a few more steps to the constabulary building, through the cobbled entry hall, out the door, and into the street. They could skirt the heart of the financial district to avoid the mobs and be back within the gates of the Hanaza before noon.

In the entry hall Jiro turned and bowed politely to the underassistant. "I can never thank you for your kindness," he said.

"Why do you mention it?"

"Well, then, good-bye for now."

"Bear yourself carefully."

"And you." The quiet tone of Jiro's voice was in contrast to his screaming anxiety to get out and be gone. They started to move to the door.

"Hey, you! Namba Cho Fire Brigade! The assistant magistrate wants to see you in here."

Jiro's body went numb. "Meet me outside," he whispered to Kinshi's back. "If I don't come right away, go to the Hanaza. Go the long way by the river."

He allowed himself to be led into the assistant magistrate's office. He was glad to sit on his feet, for it would at least hide the trembling of his legs. He bowed his head to the matting and left it there, avoiding the officer's gaze, for fate seemed determined to undo him. The assistant magistrate seated behind the table wore the crest of the heron with widespread wings—the only ranking police officer in the city who might possibly recognize Jiro.

"Where is your fire brigade?"

"Namba Cho," he replied, head still to the floor.

"No, I mean, why are they not on duty now? The whole city is in flames."

"Yes, your honor."

"Well, where are they?"

"I don't know, sir. Last night—"

"Yes, yes, I know. Last night Namba Cho Brigade performed with valor. But that was last night. Last night's bravery is not sufficient for today's crisis."

"No, sir."

"Here"—the officer brushstroked something on paper—"Take this to your head man."

Trying not to raise his head, Jiro crawled across the matting to the assistant magistrate's table. He reached up for the note.

"You're young to be a fireman."

"Yes, sir." Jiro quickly lowered his eyes.

"Have I seen you at Namba Cho before?"

"I don't know, sir." His heartbeat was likely to raise dust from the matting if the officer kept on.

"You look familiar. Perhaps I know your father?"

"I don't think so, sir. We're very low in rank at Namba Cho."

"Well, stop wasting time. Get that note to your head man immediately."

"Yes, sir." Jiro began to back out as fast as he could without seeming rude. "And thank you for your kindness."

"You found your mother safe, I hope."

"Yes, sir, thanks to you."

The officer waved his hand. He, too, was tired of politeness.

Jiro, with one motion, slid out of the room backward, into his clogs, and bowed himself out the front entrance as quickly as possible. Kinshi and Isako were not there. They must have started on ahead. Jiro broke into a trot. He could easily catch up to them.

"Hey! Namba Cho!"

Jiro ignored the cry of the underassistant.

"Namba Cho!" The policeman raced up behind him and caught his sleeve.

"Were you calling me?" Jiro asked faintly.

The policeman gave him a strange look. "You have a message for your head man from the assistant magistrate?"

"Yes. I'm just going. He said to hurry."

"Are you feeling all right? Not too tired?"

"No, no. I'm fine." How could he get rid of the man? "I'm just in a hurry to . . ."

The policeman took him by both arms and turned him around. "Namba Cho is this way," he said.

"Oh." Jiro tried to laugh. "I was just trying to avoid the crowds."

"Tell you what, son. I'll go with you." The older man patted his sword. "It's not safe, you know."

Under the fireman's coat Jiro could feel the sweat running down his arms. They began to walk toward the brigade station at Namba Cho.

"You were lucky to find your mother and brother well, weren't you?"

"Thanks to you," Jiro mumbled.

"Oh, no, it was pure luck. Do you have any idea how many people got trampled to death, not to mention those who were roasted?" He was a pleasant sort of man and talked in a pleasant tone as they walked along. Jiro tried to answer but his brain was frantically looking for a way of escape.

". . . at Namba Cho?"

"I'm sorry. What was it?"

"How many of you are there at Namba Cho?"

"Oh, not enough."

The policeman laughed. "Never enough, are there?"

They were several blocks away from the constabulary now, and the crowds were again beginning to thicken. The policeman put his hand on the hilt of his long sword, and though he kept up his chatter, his eyes were constantly sweeping the people ahead. He said something out of the side of his mouth to Jiro which the boy couldn't decipher.

"I beg your pardon."

"Don't show any fear," the policeman repeated, holding the words behind his teeth. "They are like dogs. They smell your fear."

Jiro nodded. Four or five more blocks at the most and

they would be at the station. Somewhere between here and there, he must get away.

"We're almost there," he said. "Thank you for your help. I can make it now."

"My orders"—the policeman waved his nose toward the sky—"from above." Had the assistant magistrate suspected Jiro?

"They're surrounding the fire station." For the first time the policeman's voice betrayed anxiety. Jiro could see a raggedy line of people forming around the station house. He didn't know whether to be relieved or freshly afraid.

"We'll march right up and bluff our way through. These ragamuffins are easily cowed." The officer had regained control.

Jiro nodded, still figuring how he might dart into the crowd and lose himself quickly. All the while the two of them were getting closer and closer to the fire station.

"Try to slip through that line and get to the back," the policeman was saying. "They know you, and they'll let you in."

"What about you?"

"We'll just have to see, eh?" He was a brave man, a man one would not choose to have for an enemy.

"When I give you the word, run. I can hold them off for a few minutes. It will give you time."

But abruptly the ragged line of night rovers tightened—as though someone had pulled a hidden cord. They swung about, encircling Jiro and the policeman in a quickly constricting circle.

The man drew his sword. "Run," he yelled, but it was too late. Someone from behind had grabbed the boy around the mouth, while from another part of the circle a chain whipped out, catching the policeman's sword and sending it clattering to the cobblestones.

The strong arm forced Jiro's head backward until another face was bending over, breathing into his own.

"Your promise" were all the words that Jiro heard his father say before he shoved him out of the circle.

Jiro stripped himself of the fireman's coat as he ran for the river. There was no longer any concern for whether he appeared suspicious or not. He only wanted one thing—to see Kinshi again—before he gave himself up to Okada as he had promised his father to do. His clogs pounded the paving. If he ran, there was some hope that he could intercept Kinshi and his mother before they got to the Hanaza. Nothing mattered after that.

When at last he got to the street beside the river, he could see the two of them walking slowly ahead, his friend's tall head bent over beside Isako's small form.

He began to cry out as he ran. "Kinshi! Mother! Kinshi!" He was running so fast that he had to grab Kinshi's right sleeve to brake himself. "Kinshi!"

"Don't grab him like that!" Isako screamed.

Jiro looked down at the sleeve he was holding. The arm that protruded ended in a crudely wrapped stump.

"Kinshi! What happened to your hand?"

"Ara!" replied the older boy in mock astonishment. Staring first at the stump, he thrust forward his head, and mimicking the exaggerated gestures of a puppet, he pretended to search for the missing member. He looked before him, then behind him, and to either side. He put his good left hand on Jiro's shoulder and peered down over it. At last he shook his head, and in exactly the same bantering tone he used in the boys' dressing room at the Hanaza, he said, "I seem to have misplaced the fool thing."

SIXTEEN

Debts of Honor

As Jiro and his mother walked on either side, leading Kinshi back to the Hanaza, Isako forced out the story between sobs.

"I took your father to the country—but you knew that?"

Jiro nodded.

"He told me his lungs were diseased. I believed him. Why should I not? He has always been an honest man, hasn't he? Have you ever doubted him?"

"No."

"He told me to come back to Osaka. So I obeyed. It was reasonable. Even the farmers are short of food, you know. Everything they grow goes to the daimyo or the tax collector. It's criminal. Why should a farmer's children starve while the rice brokers grow fat? Why? Why?"

Jiro shook his head. "I don't know. It doesn't seem right."

"Doesn't seem right? It's criminal; that's what it is. They had no food for me. I didn't want to leave your father. I thought he was sick. But he insisted, so I came back here. It would have been all right. I would have managed somehow. But then one day in the early spring I saw him."

"Saw who?"

"I saw your father—fat as a feast day—walking down Dotombori. Laughing he was and talking to a group of street people—not our kind. I called to him and I was sure he heard, but he pretended not to hear. He went on walking down the street, his head in the air. I would have run after him; I should have. I should have grabbed him and made him come home. I was starving, and he was laughing and happy. I-I went sort of crazy after that." She hung her head. "You remember. I'm ashamed, for your sake."

"No. You needn't be. We had both deserted you. What could you do?"

"If it had not been for this boy." She laid her hand on Kinshi's arm and began to cry once more.

"Come on, little mother," Kinshi said. "We've canceled out our debts."

"No, Jiro, don't listen to him. No one will ever know what I owe this boy. Taro went to the Hanaza to get you, but it was Kinshi who came to look for me, to get me safely home. I was with *them.*"

"Yes."

"I am so ashamed."

"I understand. Really, I do."

"But what you don't understand is what happened— the sacrifice—" Isako's voice broke. She could not go on.

"Your mother has the fault of many women, Jiro. She is incurably romantic. It was not my magnanimity but my stupidity that caused this." Kinshi lifted his arm so that the sleeve fell back from the bandage.

"No, no, he was coming after me. I was entering the house of Tsubu, the rice broker—you know the firm. Kinshi called me, but I wouldn't come back." She shook her head as though she could not believe her own actions. "I was insane—determined to steal some rice, or at least to destroy the beastly Tsubu, so that he could no longer fatten himself on the entrails of starving children. Can you understand?"

"But," Kinshi interrupted, "you must get a true picture of the scene, Jiro. You know what a fluff brain I am. I went racing toward the house all gallant hero, the blood of my warrior ancestors roaring through my momentarily noble veins. I didn't even see the policeman. And needless to say, he didn't wait for us to be formally introduced . . ."

"He cut off Kinshi's hand!" Isako's voice was shrill with the horror of it.

"He took me for a thief, little mother. And who knows? Given five more minutes, I probably would have been. He was a little hasty with his justice, that's all."

"He was a monster!"

"Do you know what I did then?" Kinshi did not wait for a reply from Jiro's frozen face. "I fainted dead away—like some sickly female. Ah, the ghosts of my ancestors must be crimson yet with the shame of it."

Jiro's hand flew to his eyes as if to shut out the unbearable scene scrawled on his brain by Kinshi's mocking voice.

"So then it was up to poor Isako to rescue me."

"Kinshi."

"She apparently marched right back into Tsubu's house, and like a magistrate demanded hot coals to stop the bleeding. When I came at last to the few senses I seem to possess, she had burned the wound like a proper physician and bound it up with a length of her own undergarment. And since it was evident that the whole lot of us were about to be arrested, she ordered two of the luckless night rovers to carry me to the constabulary and charmed a police assistant out of his padded garment to cover me with." He shook his head smiling. "A remarkable woman. I would be quite dead if it were not for her—as it is, I am very much alive." Kinshi nodded at the remains of his right arm. "I'm merely spared the ordeal of handling the feet of my father's puppets ever again."

"Oh, Kinshi." The name came out like a sob.

"Bother. The silly boy's gone soft on me."

Yoshida Kinshi, son of a line of samurai, who pick their teeth when hungry and spit contemptuously into the savage face of pain.

At last within the gates of the Hanaza, Jiro took charge. Until Okada sent for him, he would do what he could for his friend. He sent Teiji to fetch Mrs. Yoshida from her house, and Minoru to find Mochida. Wada, who obeyed as though Jiro was his senior, went to get the cold wet tea leaves and cloths for fresh dressings, and wine to ease the pain. Isako helped Jiro settle Kinshi in his quilts.

Kinshi would get more care than he wanted with both Isako and Mrs. Yoshida clucking over him, so Jiro himself went to Yoshida's dressing room.

"Pardon me for interrupting you," he called softly at the door. There was no answer. Jiro put his head into the room.

Yoshida was seated crosslegged at his table, his head in his hands.

"Master?"

The puppeteer wiped his eyes on the back of his sleeve. "Mochida has already told me," he said gruffly. "I sent for a doctor."

"If he had not gone to look for my mother—" Jiro cleared his throat. "It is my fault that . . . ."

"No," Yoshida said. "It is the nature of the boy. He has always spent his spirit the way a profligate son spends his father's wealth." He stumbled on the word father. "I feared for him. I"—he swept his arm across the table in a helpless gesture—"I fought for him with the only weapons I know. With discipline, who knows what he might have . . . ." The puppeteer shook his head as if to shake

off something that clung there. "I was not able to protect him from himself," he finished quietly.

Jiro sat in silence. How could a man like Yoshida be comforted? It was a measure of his despair that he had thus opened his heart to an apprentice. The boy kept his eyes on the matting so as not to watch the puppet master's pain.

"Does Okada know that you are here?" Yoshida broke the silence with the abrupt question.

"You know what happened between us?"

"I am Okada's eyes. It is necessary for me to know these things."

"Will he kill me?" It was a simple question. The terror that he had felt in the dark of the storehouse seemed to have vanished.

Yoshida studied him for a moment. "Why do you think he means to kill you?"

"Last night in the storehouse. I don't know. Perhaps he was only trying to frighten me."

"Perhaps he was trying to test you. He knew you would not betray *me* because of your loyalty to Kinshi. But Kinshi is not Okada's son. He had to know you would not betray him either. Perhaps he had devised a trial . . . ."

"But I ran."

"You were wrong to run."

"And I—I humiliated him. I didn't mean to do that. I was terrified, and I didn't think."

"Now that you have thought, would you betray us?" Yoshida asked softly.

For the first time in his life Jiro deliberately looked Yoshida in the face. Their eyes met like the striking of firestones.

"Never for myself," Jiro said. "But Okada has taken my father, and my mother is left alone to starve."

Yoshida was the first to lower his gaze. "Sometimes a

man must pay a heavy price to maintain his oath. But your mother may stay at the Hanaza until—until there is no more need for our deception. I can promise you that, at least."

"And Yoshida Kinshi?"

"What—what of Yoshida Kinshi?"

"If you and my father are sworn to Okada, you must understand that I am sworn only to Kinshi. No man's secret—no man's safety is more dear to me than his. But I have not betrayed Okada's secret, and I am ready to submit to whatever he chooses to do to me so long as Kinshi does not suffer. I can only guess how deeply I have offended Okada's honor," Jiro added softly. "I am sorry." Once more the man and the boy looked straight into each other's eyes. "Now, will you excuse me? I need to see how Kinshi is."

"Yes." It was all that he said.

Despite the women's protests, Kinshi was propped up regaling the other boys with a comic version of his adventures as a would-be night rover.

"Every night when I'd sneak out, I'd bump right into this police assistant. The first time I was terrified—those hooked rods of theirs are more potent than those little bamboo toothpicks I'm accustomed to—and then it occurred to me that I had done nothing wrong—at least not yet—and that all I had to do was be excessively polite. Nobody is polite enough to those fellows. Their rank is so low. I reasoned that the poor fellows would be starved for a little respect. In my politest manner—to anyone else I would have sounded like the third concubine of a minor court official in a conversation with the Emperor—I inquired about his health. A stroke of pure genius, for as it turned out, our little policeman had a terrible cough, and no one, not even his silly wife, had seemed to notice. The pitiful wretch was so grateful for my concern that it was quite touching. The next night I saw him again and went over especially to see if the cough was any better. It wasn't, and again it was so obvious that my concern had won him over that I took to looking for him each time if I didn't happen to meet him. And let me tell you it paid off. Last night I was desperately looking for my friend Isako here in the pitch-dark, and I ran smack into this policeman who was arresting everyone in sight. I was frightened out of my wits until I heard him coughing. 'Ah,' I said. 'You poor fellow. I've been looking everywhere for you. You must get out of this night air. It will be your death.' Do you know? He put his arms around me and wept? I could hardly rid myself of him in time to continue my mischief . . ."

"Excuse me for interrupting, Yoshida Kinshi." Jiro looked up startled. He had hoped for a little more time. "I was told you wanted to see me."

"Ah, Okada. You must forgive my unpardonable rudeness, but these women here wouldn't even permit me to walk across the courtyard to your dressing room. It seems I am the victim of mother love."

The chanter laughed, his funny sputtering laugh. Jiro's body stiffened at the sound. He had thought his fear gone, but apparently it had just curled up to rest in a forgotten corner of his mind.

Guided by Tozo, the blind man came over to the quilts and knelt down. He felt the cover. "You're the lazy one, lolling about in your bedclothes in the middle of the day. Doesn't Yoshida maintain any discipline at all on the west side?"

Jiro could see that Yoshida was standing in the doorway, but Kinshi did not seem to notice his father's presence, and if Okada sensed it, he gave no sign.

"We're in a lamentable state over here, Okada. I have

been thinking seriously of asking you to take me in over on the east side. The way things are going, I'll never amount to anything if I stay over here."

"I'll speak to Yoshida about it myself. But you must give me time. You know the temper of the man; he can't be approached too carefully."

Yoshida coughed.

"Yoshida," Okada said. "Come in. This foolish boy of yours doesn't know when he's well off. He's begging me to take him over to the east wing. What should I do about it?"

"If you want a nasty-tempered stallion who's"—Yoshida cleared the huskiness from his throat—"who's proved untrainable under a master horseman, you're more than welcome."

"Besides," Kinshi said gently, "what rider would waste his time with a three-legged mount?"

The master puppeteer struggled to control the muscles of his face. "Exactly," he said sternly. "The creature is useless to me. Take him with my thanks."

"If I take him like that and make something of him, you'll be sorry you let him go so cheaply, and you'll try to make me pay."

"No." The voice had recovered its usual angry tone now. "No. He's yours if you will have him."

"I have in my debt a young fellow that I'd be glad to be rid of." Okada cocked his head toward Jiro in such a way that the boy realized that the blind man had known all along where he was. "A messy matter which I won't detail—but I will give you Hanji's son Jiro in exchange for Yoshida Kinshi. You lay no further claim on this wild thing, and I'll forget the debt of the other. Is it a bargain?"

"No!" Isako cried out. "Stop this ridiculous talk, you heartless men! I don't care what his father may have said, Jiro is *my* son. I won't allow you to discuss these boys as though they were cabbages."

"It's all right, Mother." All the tightness in Jiro body began to loosen. He gave himself over to relief as a man turns over his weary limbs to the steaming water of his bath. "It's all right, really. You mustn't be upset. At the Hanaza they never talk in the way that ordinary people like you and me can understand. But they mean no harm."

"Oh, let her worry." Kinshi reached his left arm across the quilt to pat Isako's hand. "Let her worry. She deserves a little happiness."

Hellman School

3 0060 0000546 9

...ildhood
...ates, she
...apanese
... Island.
... on the
...r novels
...ok, and
...Trophy

...hildren
...d *Jacob*
...opkins,
...varded
...herine

0 0 2 0 3

FIC   Paterson, Katherine.
PAT
           The master puppeteer

Albany, NY 12208